SON OF

C000220411

The curious tale
the diamond dealer, the lottery
winner and the conman

by

Tony O'Leary

Story by Tony O'Leary
Based on the screenplay by
Tony O'Leary and Arun Kumar.

MAMBI BOOKS

Mambi
Books

First published in Great Britain by Mambi Books, 2017

The Studio, High Green, Great Shelford, Cambridge CB22 5EG

Copyright © 2017 Kimura International Development Limited.

ISBN: 978-1-903500-54-5

Tony O'Leary would like to dedicate this book to his wife Sue
for putting up with him.
Tony O'Leary would also like to thank Gerry O'Kane
for helping him on this journey,
which would not have been finished without his great
over generous help.

PREFACE

Most of this book is true as it is based around a true story. Naturally some small part, due to legalities, is fiction. All of the places are real but in some cases there is no evidence that Johnny Fay used them. Johnny Fay AKA Joe Wilkins is a relatively unknown Mr Big in the history of British crime. His reign stretched from the 1960s until the early 2000s and from London to Morocco, unmatched by many of his better-known contemporaries. His evil deeds infected and affected all the people he dealt with throughout his lifetime, having no mercy or remorse for any of his victims. Hence his nickname and title of this book – Son of Lucifer.

What is true? I prefer to leave the reader to make up their own minds.

Son of Lucifer

Chapter One
The Beginning or the End?

My psychiatrist told me that Joe Wilkins was my Mephistopheles. He peered over his glasses at me, sucking the end of his Paper Mate. Then he turned his eyes towards heaven, sighed and said, "You know, it was a Faustian pact between the pair of you."

"A what?" I answered.

"A Faustian pact, with Joe being your Mephistopheles. The favours he brought you were wealth and power but the price is normally eternal damnation of your soul since you pledged yourself to him," expanded Dr Graham.

Well there was no pledging. That wasn't the sort of shit we'd have got up to in the 70s unless you joined the funny handshake brigade.

I couldn't be bothered explaining to this over-educated prick that he wasn't Mephistopheles, but Lucifer. That's what he was known as – Lucifer, along with Joe, Johnny, smuggler, murderer, conman, grass, drug dealer and my friend. He still infected my soul but now I wanted to exorcise him.

Lucifer didn't suck me into this Faustian pact thing, but he certainly stole lives, dreams and even souls from many others. I know, I watched him do it and, God forgive me, sometimes I helped him do it. But I can prove it wasn't Faustian.

I suppose my true story was that I was one of his demons, bringing the foolhardy to his door asking for favours. But they always had to pay and always more than they ever dreamed.

Dr Graham was fairly young, one of those doctors who wanted to be your mate rather than your quack. He was also a pompous fucking know-it-all, but at least he said something from time-to-time. Someone told me the problem with psychiatrists is that they charge an exorbitant hourly rate and then only said something to put life in perspective after you'd spent five grand. It was like a grand a sentence.

But the reality was that I wasn't in for 'treatment'. I wasn't depressed or mad or psychotic, but I wanted to talk to someone and tell my story. After nearly forty years of holding my secrets I needed to get them out whether Graham believed them or not. I just hoped he didn't conclude I was a fantasist or delusional, after all the shit I'd been through it would be ironic if I ended locked up by the men in white coats.

Besides if Tony Soprano could run his New Jersey outfit while talking to a shrink and found it useful, why shouldn't I? And talking to Graham meant he had to stick to patient confidentiality rules and my tales wouldn't go any further, especially not to the Old Bill.

When I first mentioned the Krays in the same sentence as Joe I could see his eyebrow rise slightly through the gloom of his study, as he called it. He insisted on drawing the curtains in the high-ceilinged

Georgian room when we had our sessions. Naturally he'd had the place all restored: fireplace, coving with loads of twiddly bits and fancy hardwood bookshelves groaning, not only with the weight, but also the utter boredom of his collection.

Still don't know why he drew the curtains, maybe to give a sense of drama, like some sort of cabaret. Ha! He knew fuck all about real drama or even real cabaret.

The first time I came in I was lying on his leather sofa staring at the ceiling looking at a string of spider web wafting in an undetectable breeze. I started telling him about the first time I met Joe in the 60s in London's Soho. "Yeah, Joe was always a cool customer. I mean he was having a bit of a row with Ronnie and Reggie Kray about something when I first saw him – girls and clubs probably. He'd known the twins growing up in the East End and for some reason he rarely seemed worried about them."

That's when I glanced from the ceiling to look at Graham's pinched face and saw his eyebrow flick up above his trendy specs, then turn his eyes back to his notepad and scribble furiously. He was probably going to spend hours on the internet to see if there was any truth in my tale. Fuck him, it's all true but most of it hasn't been told.

That's because I'm about the only person who knew, who was told and who has figured it all out. All those old lags who went through the system and then wrote the tell-it-all books, missed Joe out. Well, they missed out the best stories about Joe and some of them they never knew. Even old Frankie Fraser, the mad cunt, knew better than to spill too much about Joe when he wrote his book in 1994.

Ha, I'd like to know what Doc Graham would have made of Frankie, whether he would have bought the bullshit of heroic romanticism that they loved their mums and gave to charity. Like Frankie and so many of his employers and enemies, the Richardson brothers and Reggie and Ronnie in that order, they're all gone now.

I'm the one who knows Lucifer's story and it took me to hell.

My name's Bill. As for my age, all I'll say is that I'm lucky to have got this old considering some of the people I worked with. I certainly wasn't muscle, never got into that. Broken bones, blood, puke, screaming and teeth wasn't something I enjoyed. In fact, I fucking hated it and Joe knew it. As a result I generally didn't see much of the rough stuff although in Joe's world there wasn't that much of it. He might have been around when Reggie and Ronnie were going at it with Charlie and Eddie, but gun fights, machetes and big brawls weren't Joe's style. It brought too much attention. He had his own way of dealing with trouble although it wasn't always successful.

No, I was more of a facilitator and manager. I had my own business lines but I had figured out which ones were low profile but brought in a regular, healthy income. That was all topped up with bonuses from Joe. He could be generous could our Joe.

Now while I might not be the sharpest axe in Frankie Mitchell's tool shed, I did have a knack with money – knowing how to invest it and how to hide it. Certainly the tax man never caught on and I doubt that even Joe knew what I had stashed away. I also managed to keep my head down when the Old Bill came sniffing around, which in Joe's case became more frequent. And, funny enough, part of the business.

There are so many stories about Joe and I've mulled them over for years. I've been like a terrier pulling each tale apart, looking and sniffing in the cracks of my memory, what Joe said, what others said.

Joe Wilkins. Family connections set him on the road to eternal damnation. But he managed to keep his feet in both the south London and East End camps being brought up in both places. Unlike his contemporaries Joe moved out of those to concentrate on central London, or more specifically Soho. While violence wasn't his preferred methodology, he wasn't above it. He was capable of it. He was six foot three and, especially in his early years, he was a heavy-set six foot three.

Then there was his style. Like I said, his family connections had educated him in style and charm. Running a good club didn't mean you had to outshine your big-paying customers, but maintaining the professional high ground was essential. I think he figured he was somewhere between Michael Caine's characters of Harry Palmer and Alfie. He certainly sported the Michael Caine horn-rimmed glasses, had Alfie's obsession with pretty girls and flash suits. He enjoyed Harry Palmer's dogged determination, school of hard knocks and appreciation of good food and wine. Above all he had both their insight into human nature.

I have come to a conclusion. I think things got over complicated one night in 1979 and while I wasn't around for the original excitement, I certainly was around for the fallout.

Yeah, Lucifer. I only found out a while ago that in Hebrew and among scholars of ancient Greece and Rome, it really means something like bright star or morning star, some sort of reference to the devil's fall from grace from Heaven. And you know, it does fit Joe because he was Satan, but he stayed operating because of his bright charm, his easy going nature but he could teach Machiavelli a thing or too. Yeah, Lucifer.

Cunt.

The sea shimmered. It was as if it shuddered with excitement of the coming morning. The sun was beginning to creep across it, but still looked as watery as that which reflected it.

Johnny stood next to an older man, both straining their eyes to make out the small silhouettes of Johnny's favourite transport. He could hear them, starting with a faint sporadic buzz, that was growing ever-louder, but all-so gradually. He and Benny had been waiting for about a half hour before the incessant buzz began, standing in the darkness, legs apart, a constant rebalancing with the gentle movement of the deck. He had entertained himself by leaning on the guardrail watching the tumbling green waves behind the stern. He never got bored of that green phosphorescence, churned up by a spinning propeller. The Mediterranean didn't always give you such a good show.

He'd learned something interesting too and Benny didn't even realise how fascinating Johnny had found the information.

"Hey Johnny, I see you like the bio-luminescence," he said in perfect English but with a clipped accent that identified him as Dutch. "Ya, some call it phosphorescence, but it's really bio-luminescence, from little things called dinoflagellates something to do with light emitting pigments or enzymes called luciferin and luciferase. Comes from Latin."

"Luciferin and luciferase, indeed. Most interesting, I'd wondered why it always fascinated me," Johnny murmured.

"What's that, Johnny?" asked Benny.

"Nah, nothing, just a private joke," he replied.

Now the ghostly green light was giving way to the golden haze of dawn. The fishing trawler was gently wallowing on a calm sea. Its beaten hull and stripped paintwork aged the boat beyond its years, just the way Benny liked it. It fitted right in when he landed in Morocco. Then two semi-rigid speed boats swept into view, ostentatiously criss-crossing their own and each other's wakes and moving fast. One could imagine the old buffalo about to be brought down by younger, fitter and faster lions.

But this was no hunt, it was business.

These two boats were Johnny's joy and his toys. And new. They were both Avon-made Sea-Riders rigid-inflatable boats, just about nineteen feet long and with two extra Perkins Marine engines. "They go like shit off of a shovel", he told everyone and sure they had cost Johnny a few bob, but he'd also managed to get a distribution deal. When some of the old faces from home who were hanging around the Costa del Sol saw them, they all wanted one. Without the add-on engines of course.

The outboard motors were powered down as the pilots, locally known as 'lancheros', carefully drifted to the trawler's side. They threw looping ropes upwards to the shadowy outlines of men on deck and were made fast.

"Hey, Pedro, glad you're keeping better time than usual," Johnny shouted down to one of the lancheros. The shadowy men were already passing parcels down to Pedro and his partner in the smaller craft. There was no weight to be struggled with and the two-foot square bales passed quickly along the trawler and into the welcoming arms of Johnny's men. Light or not, it is obvious that they're taking care that none of them end up in the water.

The two men are leaning over the side grasping the

boat's side chains watching the others graft. While the activity bustles on they pull back and turn to each other smiling.

"You've got less than twenty miles to go now, Johnny," said Benny, or 'Dutch Benny', as his imaginative contemporaries call him. He is the older and smaller of the two men. Stocky, with a fuller belly beginning to develop, the 50-year-old could look distinguished with his shock of silver hair and flecks of grey in his full beard. Unfortunately, as far as his companion is concerned, his dress sense let him down – ragged jeans, tee shirt and hippy sandals. Too much time in Amsterdam's coffee shops, thought Johnny.

"Hey and did you see those little red labels on the plastic – with the embossed rubber duck?" quizzed Benny, "Well they're our brand and are found on each ounce pack as well. We like to do it in style, huh."

Now Johnny Fay couldn't exactly be called distinguished either, although he might have thought he was, few would dare to disabuse him of the idea. He was a man of the world; mid-thirties, dark hair and sporting the must-have look of the late 1970s, sideburns and a medallion. He was, however, better dressed than his colleague in slacks and a smart open-necked shirt.

"Ah, Benny, my friend, look at this day. Sun coming up and another lesson from the master. A short boat trip across the Med in my own private fleet just in time for a bloody Mary, what can be better than that?" asked Johnny, smiling.

All the time bales are passed between trawler and dinghy's until finally the last bale is settled into its rubbery bed.

"Well there's two things to say to that," replied Benny, "First, there's nothing more I can teach you about this Moroccan/Spanish operation, my English friend. And second is that don't forget you owe the Italians five million. And that's pounds sterling, not dollars."

Johnny smiled at Benny, turned to the rope ladder stretching into the nearest dinghy and climbed down, leaping with confidence into its rocking cockpit. "Say Benny how did you know about those Lucifer thingies?" he asked looking up.

"Lucifer?"

"Y'know the bio-luminescence stuff?"

"Ah I got into this business because of my sailing and ship building skills. I went to nautical school at home, eh," explained Benny.

Johnny turned to the other dinghy's pilot and shouts, "Just follow me in when you're ready." The other driver nods.

"Hey Johnny," shouted Benny even louder as the noise of the engines go from a burble to a guttural roar, "Don't forget the Italians will want their money. Five million." He holds up five fingers.

Johnny just smiled, glanced down at the packages in the boat and then glances in the direction of the Spanish coast. Without a backward glance at Benny he takes the Sea-Rider's controls, opens the throttle and holds on.

That night was when all this really started, although I didn't know it at the time. I'm not sure if Johnny knew what he was planning exactly, but he was certainly up to something.

I was standing at the end of the pier in the old fishing port at Estepona. Through my binoculars I could see Johnny some way out, the second boat following obediently. It was travelling off to one side to avoid Johnny's wake and kept a respectable twenty feet behind.

Still about two miles out from the coast, I could tell they were passing the entrance to Estepona's new marina and heading towards me, west, a little further up the coast. Since the U-shaped marina was so new, only two years old, there was plenty of activity around it as apartments, restaurants, bars and small shops, divided over an upper and lower level were being finished off or just begun. Most places in the port had good views of the marina, so it wasn't the best place to drop off drugs.

Anyway we had somewhere much better and it wouldn't take me long in the car to get there and meet Johnny.

As I climbed to the second floor of a rather decrepit warehouse close to a rocky cove, the dinghy's still hadn't made land. It might have been a crappy warehouse but it was in a great location, looking out towards Morocco, its own private quay, part of which was under cover of another crappy warehouse. Or more strictly, a boat house.

We went for functionality and low cost rather than style. It was the one area where Johnny thought flash was not only unnecessary but could bring more problems than it solved. Besides, other little coves like Playa de El Cristo with shallow clear waters and sandy beaches attracted the tourists. Petrol-smelly water, ugly buildings and unforgiving rocks were generally enough to keep unwanted visitors at bay – so to speak.

The boat house was a few concreted-in steel uprights and cross beams covered with corrugated iron sheets, like a Nissan hut without walls at either end. Concrete jetties ran along both walls. It was more like a barn than anything else, but it did the job in keeping inquisitive eyes from seeing more than they ought. Three lorries were already waiting for the delivery.

The warehouse I was in was a little better, but then it did house our trucks and trailers and quite often, our goods. The concrete ground floor was storage and vehicle maintenance including a couple of servicing pits, while upstairs was our club and business room. Well, it had a phone, sofa, desk and drinks cabinet.

By the time Johnny was slipping into our private inlet, the sun had climbed just high enough to begin warming the top of my head. I wandered down to my silver Range Rover to take something out of the glove compartment and as I turned back to the water Johnny waved.

I walked briskly down to the boat house and by the time I got there the lancheros had already tied up and begun unloading the packages, passing them to the waiting drivers. The boss was standing hands on hips watching. He turned to me with a big smile on his face, "Ah Bill m'boy, what a great morning and I like the linen suit – very smart. You nipping down to the marina for some breakfast after business?" he asked.

"Yeah, think I might. No problems then mate?"

I should have paid more attention to his answer. With Johnny the devil, so to speak, is in the detail. It's funny what you remember years later, when pieces slot into place.

"Problems? No, no, not yet. Did you get what I asked for, Bill?"

I was glad I was prepared and had ventured already back to the car, pulling out of my pocket a small perfume-like bottle. I was smiling as I was pleased with myself for being able to sort out the order.

The bottle itself was special, a Moroccan spice or perfume bottle, I guessed. The two-inch tall glass container curved to a broad neck and was capped by an ornate brass screw top that had a small eye at the top into which was threaded a rope-woven piece of red silk. At the bottom of the glass bottle was a brass base with designs of swirling leaves, spiral galaxies and star spots, similar to the cap.

It seemed a bit over the top for knockout drops, but then I got it from one of Johnny's contacts, one of the Arab lot a bit further down the coast. Like the Chinese they like a bit of flash. The tossers call it 'bling' these days.

"Now Johnny I was told to tell you to be careful with that … Two drops in any drink and bang!" I said. I was one of the few people who called him Johnny. Ever since he had taken this new identity of Johnny Fay in Spain, it had been a struggle to avoid calling him Joe. But I learned that using Johnny rather than Jon made it easier and over time I had mastered the deception. Something to do with syllables.

Mastering deception was another thing you became good at around him.

Johnny looked to heaven, then over his shoulder at the men unloading. By now they were shoving the packets into specially designed secret compartments in the three lorries backed up to the open end of the boat house. "Keep it down Bill. We don't want everyone to know our business, now do we?"

"Sorry Johnny. Didn't think. Sorry, mate. But what do you want it for?" I didn't think much about the question. I suppose I didn't think much full stop. At least around Johnny.

"Let's say I've got a mongrel who won't shut up and the neighbours could get a little upset if they find out who done him. What did he say about traces?"

"Traces of what? Nothing, I think he said…"

Johnny never suffered fools gladly and interrupted me. "C'mon Bill stop being so stupid. Post mortem, you know when the whatsits get their hands on him to find out cause of death. What exactly do you mean 'nothing'?"

"He said there is nothing left to find, that it dissolves in a body and no trace of it can be found. That's what he said," I clarified it all quickly.

Johnny smiled, winked at me and we walked over to the Range Rover. He shouted at one of the men loading packages, "Hey Pedro mate finish off here and I'll catch up with you a little later. Some other business to take care of."

Pedro said nothing but waved.

"C'mon Bill take me for breakfast, but go to Plaza de las Flores first, there's someone I've got to see. You know in the old town."

I figured out what was going on as soon as we got to the quiet square. This was before you got too many holiday makers, especially teenagers who liked to paint a place with vomit and stagger the streets first thing in the morning having not been capable to find their way home. Actually that's not true, even today, in Estepona.

Estepona was one of the Costa del Sol's more civilized places and it was pretty, surrounded by the sea and the mountains, creating its own micro-climate with over 325 days of sunshine per year. That's what the brochures say. It has spectacular beaches which stretch out for thirteen miles and are bordered by a wide esplanade which goes from the old port all the way past the town. It has its old part with markets, squares, churches and even as the rest of Andalusia's coastline was being forested with cranes and tacky pubs, this place held on to some class.

But apart from views, Johnny had made business considerations the main reason we were based there. The new marina and the old port, where fishing was still big business, made for busy seaways, and kept us below the parapet. On top of that it was only about an hour to either Málaga or Gibraltar airport. "You have to keep your options open," Johnny would say.

And here we were in Plaza de las Flores, about five minutes from the marina. And there he was, sitting in his car, same place, same time. I called him The Slug. I'm not sure that many people particularly liked him, but Johnny had been cultivating him for some time and found the relationship beneficial.

The Slug worked in some division of the Guardia Civil, one of at least three law enforcement groups in Spain. I mean it was difficult for a Brit to keep up. Only this year they decided that the Armed and Traffic Police would be renamed the Policia Nacional and doing what exactly was unclear. Then there were local police and some sort of national investigations unit.

It wasn't so much a case of legal checks and balances, more likely that that old fascist Franco obviously believed in the ethos of divide and conquer. I suppose, this way, he kept the opposition looking over its shoulder at who else it might have to fight. Anyway the Guardia Civil was paramilitary with close links to the army and, in those days, ran Estepona. They also had jurisdiction for coasts, frontiers, ports and airports, which obviously interested Johnny. I think he also liked the idea that they had the greatest firepower.

The Slug was slouched in the driving seat of his police car, some piece of Spanish crap, arm hanging out the open window. His blue shirt was unbuttoned to the middle of his chest and his fat, chubby face already looked under sweaty stress from the climbing temperature. Yeah, he even had the greasy hair.

You know people often get upset and accuse others of using a stereotype. But in my life they weren't stereotypes but the people who I spent my time with. I mean Johnny was a stereotype and so was I, although I didn't think so at the time.

Anyway the Slug was waiting and when we pulled up alongside, he flashed a smile complete with gold front tooth, "Good morning señor, looks like another hot day in paradise, no?"

Johnny just smiled and reached into the glove compartment for an envelope. It was brown – see stereotypes. He threw it through the Slug's window and said, "Yeah it's a tough life but someone's got to do it, ain't that right?"

"Thank you, señor Johnny, I trust there are no problems?"

"Nah mate, we're off for breakfast, adiós."

Son of Lucifer

Chapter Two
Unlucky for Some

Derek Joyce was sitting hunched over his steering wheel, staring at the hazy tail lights in front. Swirling fingers of fog so typical of a winter in Dover, wrapped themselves around everything. Every now and again he could make out the slow movement of cars from another ferry ramp. Little streams of lights, some disappearing then reappearing, others flickering.

He was sitting in one of two lines of trucks waiting to be waved through by customs and like his lorry driving brethren he was sitting with his engine idling in an effort to keep out the cold air and the smog. With so many engines chugging, the fog around the vehicles had turned to smog.

The choking peasouper was so thick it had swallowed the steeply rising White Cliffs of Dover that should have been in front of him, corralling the port into a narrow strip. He loved seeing them when the ferry got closer, it gave him that warm, fuzzy feeling everyone speaks of. Pride for his nation, all that sort of malarkey.

Derek: the lorry driver, in his fifties, with a large belly overflowing from pants that never seemed ample enough no matter how many times he went up a size. Like so many, he believed the diet of the great British cafe kept a man, a man. He wasn't so sure about the grub of the continent.

He did like them French croissant things they had for breakfast – he'd usually have four or five of those in the morning along with strong coffee. The one thing he hated was that there didn't seem to a solitary hotel, service station or eating house anywhere on the continent that could make a decent cup of tea. Bloody yellow label teabags seemed to have been more successful than Hitler in conquering Europe's tea trade. Absolute shit.

His large fingers tapped the sides of the steering wheel. And you could see the ligaments in his massive forearms move, flicking the 'e' in 'Madge'. Scrolling letters tattooed the message 'Madge is my life and heart-throb' on his right arm.

He figured he wouldn't be that long waiting. Customs generally checked the paperwork had a quick word and waved you on, especially in weather like this. No one, least of all bloody civil servants, liked freezing their knackers off. Then it was up the A2 and he'd be in London in time for the missus to make him a fried breakfast.

Derek had been making this trip for years. When he'd started driving lorries you had to off-load your freight into the hold of a ship and someone else picked it up on the other side – no trips abroad. It took a few years after the advent of Dover's roll-on, roll-off freight ferries in 1965 to get into the continental runs and a lot of hassle in the beginning, but it had been worth it. Over the years the duty free 'care packages' he brought home had turned into a nice little pension pot. Mind you this job was definitely a big contributor to his pension and would go some way to paying for that nice little bungalow down in Torquay. His extra cargo was a profitable sideline and one that he only occasionally was asked to carry, which was fine with him.

The port had been getting busier and busier since he'd started, which was okay too since it kept the customs guys busier too and they tended to preoccupy themselves with new drivers and hauliers rather than an old hand like himself. He'd noticed that with the opening last year of the Hoverport at the Western Docks, after they'd spent years reclaiming 15 acres of land from the sea, they'd been even more stretched.

His thoughts were interrupted as he inched his way to the front of the queue and the lorry in front rumbled past some officers. He wound down his window, a sheaf of papers in hand to pass over the officer on duty as he normally did. This time however, two customs and excise men, used their torches to wave him into the examinations' shed way off to the left. "Just routine," he said to himself, "Nothing to worry about."

Most of the officers wore regulation dark blue uniforms with varying amount of gold buttons, pips and braid to show how far up or down the superiority league they were. Only a few wore high visibility jackets but most had some form of hand torch.

Derek was busy walking around his lorry, appealing to any customs officer who would speak to him that they were putting him behind schedule and what a waste of their time this was. He didn't notice the brown Granada Mk2 2.8i GL manual lumber up to the shed and two men get out.

The driver, Detective Sergeant Elder, was about 30 had fair hair but a face that could only be described as hard. His blue eyes were cold and his demeanour said nothing but business. His rain coat was wrinkled down the back, his tie lose and a drip dry shirt displaying this morning's hurried boiled egg indicated that fashion was not his preoccupation.

An older man got out of the passenger seat. The man, somewhere in his forties, acted more assuredly and seemed in less of a rush, as befitting a Detective Chief Superintendent. Mr Farringdon had black hair with grey streaked through it giving him a regal air. In spy novels he would be described as steely-eyed and square-jawed, while Barbara Cartland would have called him 'desirable'. He smoothed the back of his dark blue Crombie coat and walked determinedly towards an approaching customs officer.

This man was obviously in charge. His dark blue uniform was immaculately pressed, the two parallel sets of four gold buttons polished on his double breasted jacket and not a speck of dust on his white topped peaked cap. The braid on his peak and crown seated above the portcullis badge on its front, all perfect.

"You're Detective Chief Super Farringdon, I take it," asked the uniformed officer.

"Yes and you are…?"

"I'm Chief Preventive Officer Macey. What are we looking for then?" his arm with three gold rings at the end of his sleeve gesturing towards the lorry.

"We are not 'looking'," responded DS Elder rather too curtly. Macey raised an eyebrow. "We know it's there on the back of that lorry… if my information is right," continued Elder.

"Information? From whom?" asked Macey.

"Joe bloody Wilkins, that's who," replied Elder. "Try and make the search look good, will you?"

For twenty minutes ten customs officers scurried around the lorry, looking in every available place, while Derek watches on, becoming whiter by the minute. "So much for Torquay," he thought to himself.

Then there was a shout. "Got something here, sir," an officer called to Macey. He wandered over to the three men who were a little way off and said, "I'd say we're looking a street value of maybe three million in cocaine. We're still pulling it out".

"Okay get on with the official bit then," said Macey.

As Derek is led away in handcuffs, Farringdon can just about hear the mumble of legal warnings, "Under section 139 of the Customs and Excise Management Act 1979, we are seizing these goods and…"

Elder turns to Macey with a wide smile and says "That'll make you look good, won't it?".

Farringdon says nothing, no flicker of emotion on his face. Macey looks at him, nods, turns on his heels and walks away to join his men still searching Derek's lorry.

"Well boss, that's three loads within five months. Looks like Joe's on the ball, not bad information, eh?" Elder smiles again. Again Farringdon says nothing and waits for Macey to walk out of earshot.

Farringdon had worked with Elder before. He wasn't in the same division, he was what Elder would refer to as the 'shadow men' – Special Branch. He knew Elder was competent but he was a little too sure of himself and with something of a big gob.

He turned and looked at Elder. "You do have a big mouth, Elder. Please don't discuss our sources in front of the grunts. Remember Joe works for us, not them. And it's sensitive so let's keep it that way, okay? You should know how delicate this situation is." He turned on his heel and started back to the Granada. Elder hesitated for a second then tries to catch up with his boss, internally kicking himself for such a basic mistake.

"Sorry guv, it won't happen again," he apologises, but Farringdon says nothing. Instead he thinks to himself, "Guv? Ever since that fucking Sweeney started on TV, they all got to use 'guv'. Idiots."

Chapter Three

Benny Considers Retirement

I could see Johnny pausing outside Benny's villa, standing in the road. He was taking in the night air, a quiet moment of contemplation that I'd noticed he often did before evening business meetings. He was clutching a large leather briefcase, the sort I'd seen my teacher use, with two buckles and a click lock in the centre of the lip. He didn't know I was watching. I was sitting in my car down the road, waiting to meet him here at Benny's.

I'd sat in the car since I thought there was a bit of a chill in the night air. But as Johnny said, it was still pretty warm and certainly better than England in winter.

He cocked his head back and looked up at the clear night sky. There were stars everywhere and for Johnny the galaxy was his domain too. Behind him rose a shadow of mountains that was the backdrop to the town. He took another deep breath, then turned to a wrought iron gate in the middle of a six foot high whitewashed wall and entered.

I met him at Benny's front door as he weaved his way along a paved path between exotic plants and trees. I could catch the heady scent of jasmine somewhere in the night air. I loved jasmine. It intermixed with the harshness of the chlorine from the huge swimming pool Benny had at the back of the house.

"Ah there you are Bill," greeted Johnny as he skipped up the steps to the front door and gave it a quick rap.

The front door led into the single storey part of the house. The two story part had a snug with an open fire and a spiral staircase to an upstairs bedroom suit with en-suite. On the ground floor

Before we could talk any further the heavy teak door opened and Benny looked out, drink already in hand. "Gentlemen, welcome. Come in. Drinks I presume?"

We followed Benny down an echoing hallway and into a large lounge with floor-to-ceiling windows that normally looked out to the pool and garden beyond. Tonight it framed only blackness.

Unlike so many properties in Spain, I noticed that Benny liked rugs. The clatter of our footsteps softened when we entered his living room – obviously acquisitions from Morocco over the years. He had a huge living room at the back of the house, open plan with log fireplace and dining area. The living room also had split levels. I could see into the kitchen, fully equipped in stainless steel, all modern appliances.

Benny gestured to the cloth sofas and armchairs and turned to his bar area, reached below the top and pulled up some whiskey glasses. Before he could pour anything, Johnny shouted, "Whoa Benny, try this since it's been such a good day for me." He pulled out a dark green bottle of Henroit champagne, and began to take off the foil and started to work the wire and cork. "Don't worry Benny, I made sure it was chilled before I walked down here."

Benny smiled raising his crystal cut glass a little, "I'll just finish this scotch." He brought over two champagne flutes, picked up the bottle and gave a little whistle. "Must have been a good day, Johnny. It's Cuvée des Enchanteleurs a very nice vintage. Well, I'll pour."

But that was the end of the idle chit chat, Benny wanted to talk business. "My partners have been in touch and they say they want their money by Friday, so how's it going?"

Johnny took a sip of champagne, savoured it for a second then said, "Well a little shipment left this morning and it should be delivered in less than four days, so all's well with the world."

Benny smiled, then shook his head, "I hope so, we've had a few deliveries go awry into England lately. Your customs guys are getting luckier, so it will be good to see how you fare."

"Never fear, I've been at this a long time, I know how to get it through," Johnny laughed. Johnny had been smuggling since the early 60s. When he and I first started doing business it was smuggling a bit of grass and resin – the collie herb, Mary Jane. But soon after we started together Johnny confided in me that he had cut his teeth in getting one over on Her Majesty's Customs and Excise officers by bringing in porn from Holland,

and cheap perfume. It was something I later took over as the margins became less attractive for Johnny, who was now big time. For me, I could avoid the nasty boys and law enforcement began to look on that business as not worth their while. There were bigger fish to fry.

"Now Benny, do the Italians know I'm your customer? You did say to me that I should be the silent partner with regard to them," he asked.

"Oh no, I didn't mention you at all. They have always dealt with me and don't like new faces, so I just forgot to say who found the buyers and who was moving the stuff. Myself and the Italians have a history, yes…? But when we complete this I will make an introduction as they'd be impressed to see who can move this amount. I'm considering early retirement and this business seems to be a younger man's game these days," he confessed.

"Bollocks, Benny, you're not that old a fart. Besides we did a great morning's work," joked Johnny. He got up from the sofa, skipped up the three steps to the bar and picked up the ice cooler emptying it into a champagne bucket. He screwed the champagne into the ice, then searched for another flute.

"Hey Bill, show Benny your latest flash acquisition, mate," encouraged Johnny.

Benny turned to me with an interested look on his face. "Acquisition? That sounds expensive. What have you got?"

I rolled up my shirt sleeve, turned my arm to hold

up a new Rolex. "Business has been good Benny, so I thought I'd invest it and bought this baby." Benny moved closer to look at it, while Johnny poured another glass of bubbly in the fresh glass, glanced back then pulled the Moroccan perfume bottle from his front pocket.

I wasn't sure at the time that it was the perfume bottle, but I certainly was later.

"Ah it's a, it's a Rolex Oyster Perpetual 1002 in fourteen carat yellow gold. Bought it in London from a dealer. He says it was made in 1951 and the way I see it, these are always a tradeable commodity, means I can always have a few grand on me, y'know," I stuttered.

Benny whistled for the second time. "You're a quiet man, Bill but that hides your smarts, I think," smiled Benny.

By this time Johnny had wandered back to the sofa and handed Benny the fresh glass of champagne. "Now you have to drink this and toast our future, okay?" he said.

"Sure Johnny, I do love this stuff. But, eh, your contacts do have the funds ready don't they, I don't want to upset my Italian friends."

"Of course, Benny boy. These lads have deep pockets and when they take delivery, then we'll all be well in profit." He smiled again, "Drink up boys."

"Proost," saluted Benny as he threw his head back and emptied his glass in one gulp. Johnny looked at me, smiled that smile and winked. I finished mine, looked at them both, stood up and showed myself to the front door.

Chapter Four
Bye, Bye Bentley

It wasn't long after our 'celebratory' drink with Benny that I made my way to London ahead of Johnny. As he liked to remind me, not infrequently, I was the man for the small practicalities in life. What he meant was, for the stuff he couldn't be arsed to do.

I always found coming back brought conflicting emotions. While no one had a dislike for me, being around Johnny could bring unknown complications into your life. But I missed the old pubs – the smell of stale beer, the sticky carpets, the tuneless piano in the corner and the wanker who thought he was the locals' answer to Elton John. I missed the food too, up to a point. But Soho always seemed the same, grubby, but my grubby, and I still knew some of the best clubs around – you always knew someone who had fingers in many pies.

On the other hand I lived in some comfort in Spain. The girls were a better class. And I loved the weather, there. I found the cold and the damp really got into my bones when I went home and going to the pub wrapped up like Scott of the Antarctic always turned a few heads.

But then I was never in London for that long and I looked at it as an all-expenses paid holiday complete with top-notch hotel.

This trip was not a change in business for Johnny, it was simply a step up in scale. He wasn't stupid. He knew if customs and the Old Bill were on the lookout for his tip-off of cocaine, then they wouldn't be paying so much attention to anything else. That's when we brought in Benny's consignment. This was only part one of his plan.

Like I said about Johnny, he knew what made people tick. He managed to get them to believe that the disastrous consequences of a project was because they had thought of it, they had masterminded it. Funny how he still made money, but kept his neck out of the noose. Well, most of the time.

This time he was to make big bucks. Not only was he getting a considerable wedge from what the politicians like to call 'law enforcement', but he was making a killing from those he planned to 'fix'.

The job was an easy one. We relied on the greed of the dealers – make them an offer they couldn't refuse a most reasonable price, then leave the constabulary to clean up the mess before they got to examine all the goods. We get top money, the Old Bill get a small amount of gear, but enough for a judge to take the moral high ground and chastise them with double-digit sentences. If there was any difference in the quantities of gear the dealers were expecting and what the prosecution offered the court, they figured the coppers had nicked the rest. Fairly common practice back in those days.

Plus they all knew Joe Wilkins. In London it was Joe and his reputation for shady dealings that always preceded him. Being a contemporary of the Krays and

Richardsons and having done business with both gave him a name. After all, he survived them both and wasn't banged up either. He was also no stranger to the drugs game. No, Joe's name got him in most places.

As in Spain, we had a legitimate little business based down in Walworth. Joe was born in south London and liked to keep in touch with his home turf, as he called it. In reality Walworth was the Richardson's stomping ground back in the day. They had a scrap metal yard, while Johnny had bought a little yard off East Street, in Walworth Place. He hadn't used it much when he first got it, but now it was an inconspicuous investment in a busy area and no one knew who owned it. It was always out on temporary lease to someone.

East Street market might not have been what it once was, but Wednesday and Saturdays saw hundreds of stall holders flaunt their wares, right down East Street to Portland Street. It was an area that traditionally didn't ask too many questions because everyone was up to something. He also got a kick out of it being within a stone throw's distance of the Labour Party headquarters.

It was a grungy area, filled with locals who could trace their families back to markets, river trade and fighting for King and country across the empire since the empire started. Ironically they were now increasingly forced to share space with growing numbers of immigrants who found in the Southwark Council welcoming arms for housing asylum seekers. What those mugs didn't know when they landed at Heathrow is that the housing was in the Aylesbury Estate. Built in the 1960s it was maze of multi-storey shit holes, ideal for rape, murder, drug dealing and muggings. Years later Prince Charles pronounced it as the worst high rise housing estate in western Europe. No arguments from me.

I was meeting Johnny as he came off the plane at Heathrow but first I had a bit of stock management to sort out.

The yard itself wasn't huge but could easily accommodate four or five lorries, a couple of cars if packed in and around the small office and toilet in a few brick, single storey outhouses. The brick walls were easily tall enough to keep people out, helped by a healthy helping of razor wire along the top. The heavy double black wooden gates were as tall as the walls, also wire-topped.

Apart from that we had a Frank. He was the bloke that looked after the yard and could watch it from his flat across the road. He could keep an eye on the yard without having to be in it and knew better than to sniff around or ask questions when myself or Johnny turned up. He was also an old boxer and still drifted over to the Old Kent Road and into the old Thomas a Becket gym to watch the young lads train. He had trained there when the Krays were members.

The three lorries we had filled in Costa del Sol, were sitting locked up in the yard, parked up with a fancy-looking VW Camper van we owned. We'd bought the T2 model, the one without the split wind shield.

I went to each of the trucks, scrambled around trying to get access to the secret compartments and shifted the packets around, all with their embossed rubber duck red labels on the plastic. "Only twelve packets to Blighty," Johnny had directed. "Never put all your eggs in one basket, Bill, m'boy."

I'd left two packets in one of the lorries' secret compartments and two in another. I moved the rest into the VW Camper van and its own hidey-hole in a sealed sub-section of the water storage tank. Opening the gates, I got into the kombi and drove it out to the street, pausing only to honk and let Frank now it was time for him to close the doors.

I parked the Camper van at one of our other safe spots and made my way to Heathrow.

It was its usual nightmare. Crowds of people moving in one direction and the other, pausing, looking up, putting bags down, looking at tickets, staring at shop windows, squinting at information boards as the names and numbers clacked like a brood of hens. I hated the place. I always preferred coming by boat if I could. Johnny, of course, liked the glamour of being recognised at the check in desks in Málaga and Heathrow as one of those frequent fliers.

We met at one of the bars, greeted each other as if we hadn't met in years and made our way to the taxi rank in front of the terminal. "Everything go well, then, Bill?" asked Johnny.

"Naturally, left a load in the VW Camper van, four in the lorries and we're all ready to go," I replied.

There was his trademark grin again, as we swept through the swing doors to the bitter winds outside. Then I noticed it fade.

Sitting at the head of the taxi rank wasn't a black cab, the old Austin FX4 I that always warmed my heart when home, but a nasty brown Granada. It wasn't because Johnny was a car fan that he'd stopped smiling, it was the company the car kept.

Leaning on the Granada was Detective Sergeant Elder and Chief Superintendent Farringdon. I hadn't seen Farringdon for a few years but he still was something of an imposing figure and dressed immaculately, unlike Elder who always looked like he'd been dragged through a hedge backwards.

Standing with them, smoking a cigarette, was someone I didn't recognise. He was stockier than either Elder or Farringdon and his hair was thinning on top. He looked older than Elder but younger than Farringdon, with a world-weary face. A mister in-betweenie.

"Hello boys," sneered Elder. "Meet Chief Inspector Hargreaves. As Mr Farringdon here is a busy man, Mr Hargreaves will be dealing with you two."

"Well Joe, how's 'bout you and monkey McFadden take a little trip with us," spat Elder as he stared at me. I said nothing. That was always the rule, say nothing when Johnny was doing business. Not unless he asked you. It was a bit like not listening unless you were expected to – it simply made life a lot easier. At least to my stress levels.

"Tut, tut, Mr Elder," said Johnny smiling. It was that all-lips, no-eyes thing that he does. "You should know that there's a time for aggression but this isn't it. We've no disagreement, all-in-all that sort of attitude doesn't seem right. In fact at this particular juncture it's downright inappropriate."

I glanced at Farringdon. He was just standing there with his hands in his dark blue Crombie watching this exchange with a faint smile playing on his lips. The look had seen it all before, fiery young sanctimonious copper and Lucifer. Wind-up merchant Lucifer, cheeky Lucifer, assured Lucifer – always watching how he might make it play out.

Hargreaves said nothing either but just held the back door open and nodded to Johnny to get in. Elder shoved me into the front seat and told me to shut up with a stare. The silent Hargeraves went around to the other back passenger door and got in, while Mr Farringdon got in after Johnny. Elder got into the driver's seat and turned around.

I could see Johnny in the mirror, looking somewhat pained at being squeezed between the two older, large men.

Elder started, "Alright then Joe, what you got for me? And remember, you fucking waste my time with shit and…"

Johnny interrupted, looking him in the eye, "So how did you do at Dover the other day then?"

It was then Hargreaves spoke, in a quiet voice that

somehow sounded like a snake, "Listen, you. If it wasn't for us putting your deal to Mr Farringdon in the first place, you'd be doing time, so don't come the hero here."

Elder chipped in, "New passport. New identity. Immunity from prosecution. And get paid for it! Can't get better than that, can you Johnny Fay? Or maybe you would prefer to return and face charges as Joe Wilkins."

The double-act went on with Hargreaves continuing. "And have no illusions Joe. We can always report to Mr Farringdon here that we can't work with you and he'll have a chat elsewhere to sort this problem out."

Mr Farringdon just stared at Johnny and said nothing. I could see Johnny's smile had long gone and there was a sigh of inevitability. "Alright, alright, I get it, just let's move on."

The next day me and Johnny were down at the yard in Walworth. He hadn't said much about our meeting at Heathrow and that was just fine with me. We both knew what was involved, after all it wasn't the first time Johnny had gone through this wringer and he always managed to get out of it. It was one of those miserable damp days that Johnny's demeanour seemed to reflect.

I was sitting in the passenger seat of Johnny's new motor. Apart from the yard logistics I had been sent over to do, Johnny had also wanted a new toy. One to show off. It would be secreted away in the same place the VW Camper van was now sitting when we weren't in the country. And since Johnny liked flash, it was.

The brand new V12 Jaguar XJ12 5.3 litre had an engine that roared. British racing green with a black vinyl sunroof, rubber bumpers topped with decorative chrome, flush door handles, twin headlights and split grill with narrow vertical vanes. It was a showstopper.

Johnny was standing close by the lorries, when two cars pulled into the yard. They were work cars, four doors, big engines but ugly. British Leyland, of course, but apparently it was now called BL – that didn't make the cars any better. Two heavies got out of the nasty red Austin Princess. In behind it pulled a 1977 Rover SD1 with the imaginative colour of brown. It was hard to believe it had won European Car of the Year in 1976 but Bentley, the guy we were here to do business with, had evidently bought into the bullshit. That was a good sign for us.

I watched from the Jag. Johnny nonchalantly moved to the lowered tailgate of the first lorry where there was already a split bag of coke sitting in a leather briefcase.

The two heavies stood by the Princess. Both of them wore Harrington bomber jackets and denim jeans. Only one, however, was a skinhead but he did come complete with bright red Doc Martin boots. Both were ugly – flat noses, high foreheads, the usual sort of thing. Both chewed gum and stood with their arms stretched downwards, hands over their groin.

They shouted, 'No imagination'.

But when Bentley got out of the Rover and slowly walked over to Johnny, it was a different matter. I never knew him as anything but Bentley, but he oozed menace.

According to our info, he'd made his name with Millwall's 'F' Troop – no mean feat for a black man among England's most violent firm of football hooligans. Then he'd started doing business in Deptford and Brixton. He was not to be messed with. But then that never worried Johnny.

Not only was Bentley the only black man in the yard, but he was the largest man in the yard and his saunter screamed cock-of-the-walk. Like his Princess boys, he wore jeans, held up by a tooled leather belt with a devil's buckle and Green Flash runners. His stocky torso was clothed in an expensive Donegal tweed jacket, the white shirt's lapels overlapping the jacket's collar.

In his right hand he grasped a metal briefcase. I nearly sniggered, this was all too Hollywood.

His driver walked two steps behind and while he was the same large build as the Princess boys, he wore a smart grey suit, white shirt and blue paisley tie. Only his hair looked as if it needed some expert styling, lying languidly over his collar. I noticed he had something of a bulge in his lower back, distorting the lie of his jacket. Another shooter.

Johnny smiled. "Alright Bentley. Nice to see that you've brought your readies. Have a taste of this my son," he said as he turned to the packet, scooped some white powder onto the end of a flick knife and turned back to Bentley.

Bentley placed the case on the tail of the lorry and opened it. Johnny glanced in at neatly piled bundles of fifty pound notes, while Bentley took the knife from Johnny. He snorted the coke up his nose and then wiped the blade clean with his finger, rubbing the detritus around his gums. He threw his head back and breathed out heavily.

When his head came back down, his face was smiling. "Sweet. Very clean. That should cut up well. Okay tell your delivery boys to bring it to this address," he whispered, handing Johnny a note of paper.

Johnny had stopped smiling and looked Bentley in the eyes. "Now, Bentley, I don't have to check this case do I son? I don't have to worry about upsetting my partners, do I?"

This time it was Bentley's turn to smile, his perfect white teeth overloading his face. "C'mon Joe, we wouldn't have lasted long in this game, if we cheated each other, would we, mate?"

Johnny said nothing but folded the metal case shut and walked over to the Jag. Slowly, deliberately he opened the car's boot and placed the briefcase in it face down. He walked around to the driver's seat, got in and started the car revving the 5.3 litre engine. As he slowly pulled away passing Bentley, he lowered the one-piece window, "Be lucky son", turned to me smiled and screeched out the gates, turning left.

I knew they were there. Down one end of Walworth Place were two cars, one of which was a brown

Granada. As we turned right towards Portland Street, a blue Bedford van with British Gas Corporation livery turned into Walworth Place and then into the yard.

We both knew what was about to happen.

The side sliding door was pulled back. At the same time the two back doors burst open and eight police men piled out. They'd be the usual Liquorice Allsorts – a couple of plain clothes long-haired yobs from the drugs squad, four from D11 in their poncy blue berets carrying heavy Lee Enfields and assuming the position. I expect two uniformed cops followed on waving whatever was left over in the armaments box.

The two cars that had been sitting at the bottom of Walworth Place, had moved up the street and followed in behind the van. DS Elder leapt out of the passenger seat, with a satisfied look in his face and waving a Webley & Scott revolver in Bentley's direction.

By this time we were two streets away, heading down Morecambe Street, thinking we well out of it. A car pulled out from the kerb and blocked us in.

Johnny looked at me, said nothing but drew breath through his teeth. He got out.

It was an unmarked police car. One man was already out and moving towards Johnny, while the other had a radio in his hands. They both did a double-take when they spotted Johnny.

I could hear the copper on the radio. "We've stopped the car and got two here, sir."

He paused for second, looking at Johnny again. "Excuse me sir, but are you Johnny Fay?" Both coppers looked at each other and shook their heads.

Johnny only nodded, standing with his hands on his hips. The radio crackled again. "Okay, my boss wants to speak to you."

I have to say I hadn't expected that. My heart was pounding, but when I heard that it was my turn to smile. I got out, as Johnny took the radio stretching the coil from the unmarked car.

I could hear Elder, "We're going through the lorries but it's been a little disappointing. I thought we'd get more than this."

"You have four kilos, haven't you. Besides don't worry, there's more to come." Johnny turned and looked at me, a smile growing. "You have my word, Mr Elder."

A few more indistinguishable words passed between them, before Johnny passed the radio back to the policeman. Johnny waited beside the police car, while the copper took a further message. "Okay Mr Fay, he said for you to… fuck off!"

"Good day gentlemen," said Johnny as he tipped his hand towards his brow, returned to the car, revved the engine and skidded down the road.

Chapter Five
Hello Luxury

Johnny was leaning on his Range Rover, leg folded against the door, his back supported by the half open window. His eyes, hidden by sunglasses even though it was still early morning, scanned the people passing. He knew he shouldn't be parked where he was, but he knew the police at the airport. He had made a point of it.

His car was at the end of the taxi rank just next to lines of coaches that were parked diagonally nose-in, facing the front of the main Málaga Airport terminal.

He'd watched Málaga Airport get busier and busier over the last few years, but at least he wasn't anywhere near the new terminal that catered for the fish and chip brigade, all those new package deal tourists from England and elsewhere. It brought him some business, but a little too much bad feeling in some Spanish quarters. No, this was for scheduled air traffic but like most 60s terminals it sported a wall of glass doors in front of him, while the rest of it rose as a headstone of windowless grey concrete.

He had been there about twenty minutes. All shapes of people going in and coming out – those dressed in especially bad shorts and blindingly bright shirts, others in business suits.

But then he could see what he was waiting for, even through the throngs. She was an impressive sight. Long blonde hair, early 30s, about six foot tall, a figure that said "I know you want me" and the practised walk of a model. That was the little hip swagger, one foot carefully placed in front of the other.

What she was wearing wasn't from a Paris catalogue, though. It was Iberia Airway's "winter collection" as she called it. The light brown knee-length skirt hid her long shapely legs, the five buttoned brown waist-length jacket camouflaged her pert breasts. The blouse, a brown and white check, peeped above the jacket's breast line and the collar overlapped it. Around her long neck was the white scarf with a huge yellow and orange IB logo, stretching down to a bland collection of eight coloured hoops, dull yellows, oranges, duller browns and a solitary blue. But her blonde hair managed to shine through the brown beret faced with another Iberia trademark.

Still, Johnny thought to himself, it's better than that old blue uniform head wear that looked like a cross between a jockey's racing cap and a metropolitan police helmet. Highly unattractive.

She pulled behind her an airline bag with a metal briefcase strapped to the top. At the sight of Johnny she broke into a trot and as she reached him, dropped the bag behind her and threw her arms around his neck.

"Hello darling. Good flight, no trouble I hope," greeted Johnny after he extricated himself from the embrace and passionate kiss. "No, no Trouble. Straight through as always, honey."

They got into the Range Rover and drove away from the airport, west towards Estepona and home. Home for Johnny Fay in those days was a bright, white apartment that looked down to the marina, on its broad balcony a collection of chairs around a glass table. Inside typical dark wooden Spanish furniture was to be found in every room.

But Johnny had other things on his mind rather than décor. He had closed over the bedroom window shutters allowing only a stream of light to enter. His king-size bed with an ornate and overwhelming headboard was a nightclub stage, the beam of sunlight illuminating the scattered contents of the metal case. Bentley's tightly bound bundles of fifties had made their way home, at least to Lucifer's home.

But Estelle Jorgenson knew how to get what she wanted and as Johnny licked his lips and felt the cash, she dropped her skirt, unbuttoned her blouse, leaned over his back with her blonde hair covering his face. "Johnny, I've never been fucked on a bed of cash before."

It was another two days and 15 bottles of champagne later, before the aphrodisiac effect of the cash wore off and Johnny emerged to do business again.

He had already arranged the villa viewing before Estelle had returned to Spain and while he heard it was something of a special property, he had no idea just how special until he saw it. The plot, he knew, was big and off the Calle el Cid, but it was when he drove up the short avenue lined with palm trees to an imposing whitewashed arch with a stone coat of arms sunk into its apex, that he knew it was special. The wrought iron gates lay open and grand lamps hung from chains to either side. He drove into a courtyard and pulled up next to the two storey, whitewashed "cottage", noticing that the impressive front double doors of heavy oak with metal rivets already open.

Mark Lufton, the estate agent, was standing at the top of the marble steps shuffling, clutching a clipboard and looking nervous. He was about five feet eight dressed smartly, out of respect for his clients, a light jacket, open-necked blue button-down shirt, a pair of white trousers and a pair of fashionable brown leather moccasin. He seemed to have a habit of running his hand through his short spiky dark hair.

As Estelle and Johnny got out of the Range Rover, she looked up and squealed, "Look Johnny it has its own bell tower," gesturing to the square tower that adjoined the house and started the archway row, that led to private gardens and swimming pool.

"Ah Mr Fay, my name is Mark," he stretched out his hand. Johnny shook it and looked around him. "Quite a place, Mark," he answered.

"Yes, part of it was built in the 16th century but then a Hollywood star who was filming in Africa bought it in the 1950s and extended it," Mark pattered.

The main house was intriguing. After a few small rooms to either side, it entered what might be considered a lounge. Not massive but certainly impressive, a ceiling that extended to this single storey roof with red pine beams extending to the apex. At one end was an antique manteled fireplace with a free-standing chimney, while to either side of it were three steps that wound around the back of the fireplace and up to a corridor that accessed three more bedrooms.

"As you can see, Mr Fay, it's been built with Andalusian, Arabian and Mexican influences, it's especially noticeable outside," said Mark. "The architect was Manuel Camisuli."

After investigating the bedrooms and opulent bathrooms all with carved doors, tiles from Seville and Italian marble fittings, they came back to the lounge and at the other end of the room, under curved arches towards the kitchen, dining room and out to the poolside area.

"Hmm, this is something," commented Johnny as he looked down along a forty foot by twenty room open-aired on one side, the grass lawn and half-sized Olympic swimming pool, farmed by delicate arches. The garden and pool area was over half an acre with faux Grecian pillars, exotic trees and bushes and surrounded by walls and self-contained bedrooms in the form of small Spanish villas. Inside the room, the ceiling stretched to the apex of the roof, the floor of brown Spanish tiles interrupted by ceramic heraldic shields. Halfway down the wall was an arched dark oak door leading back into another garden at the back of the house and to either side windows. It was dominated by a priory-style table that could seat twelve people. By the door coming down from the house were a few steps, while to the side of the doorway stood a fully stocked bar.

"It's a bit like something out of the High Chapperall," laughed Johnny, noting but not saying that each ground floor window was guarded by heavy black wrought iron grilles. He turned to Estelle, "Darling will get the bag from the car?"

Estelle swung around, her long blonde hair bouncing over her shoulders, coyly glanced back at Mark and board-walked her way towards the house.

"Does your wife swim Mr Fay?" he asked, his eyes following her across the tiles.

Johnny smirked. Time for business. "She's not my wife, I'm not married and for this deal it will be Mr Wilkins, Mister Joe Wilkins, buying the house, you understand mate?"

Mark, abruptly turned to Johnny and looked more closely at him. Mark was in his late twenties, a grammar school boy, certainly not stupid but no silver spoon either. He'd been brought up in a rough part of Liverpool and had watched the local wide boys operate, though always at a safe distance and by maintaining cordial relations. He was in Spain to make money and the one thing he'd been good at in his grammar school was Spanish and maths. And being good with the chit chat just came naturally.

"Of course. Client confidentiality is my speciality," replied Mark, licking his lips.

"Like I said she's not my wife, so not even she knows about Joe Wilkins, understand? And on that note how much for cash?" asked Jonny staring at him.

Mark moistened his lips more vigorously this time. "Eh, cash? You mean you want to buy the place for cash? Outright?" His voice slightly elevated at this last word.

" Yeah, C-A-S-H. That's it spelt out for you. What I need you to do is pass that offer to your client. How you handle the details is up to you, my offer is in cash," emphasised Johnny.

"Well forgive me for saying this, but you do realise we're talking eight hundred thousand pounds, sir," queried Mark.

"No, we're talking cash, we're talking seven hundred thousand. I certainly didn't think it was pestas. And I want to move in by Thursday next week. Is there a problem?"

"No problem at all, sir. My client has had it up for sale a long time so there shouldn't be any problems at all," said Mark.

Estelle had wandered back to Johnny's side and passed him the briefcase. Johnny turned from the pool and Mark and walked back to the table. He upended the bag and said, "There you go seven hundred thousand pounds, crisp fifties all wrapped up for you. Don't go spending all your bonus at once, Marky-boy. Being thrifty is a useful virtue. I'm sure we'll do business again."

"Any time Mr Fay," replied Mark carefully.

Johnny looked him in the eye, patted his arm, smiled and said "Good boy, quick learner. I like you. I'll be in contact."

Chapter Six
Wakey, Wakey Benny

People rarely think of what's happening anywhere else when you're having fun. Someone might be winning millions on the spin of a roulette wheel in Monaco, while a teenager is getting his kneecaps blown off in a back entry in Belfast. The businessman could be signing the biggest contract of his life envisaging his new Porsche, while some poor kid could be watching his parents cough their last breath in a mud hut in a cholera-struck village in the Congo.

I know I never thought about it, least-ways not until lately. I know Johnny never thought about it, or at least if did he kept it well hidden. I suppose he might have, since he was so good at figuring people out and all the angles, but it certainly wasn't from any empathy viewpoint.

The way I figure it, about the same time when Johnny got back from the airport with Estelle, Dutch Benny got a visit.

Well, he would have had a visit had he still been alive.

And that was it, the balloon went up. I'm still not sure who found him. It could have been a maid, it could have been the pool man or the gardener. It could have been Carlos. I'll come to him in a minute, but I didn't know him then.

While Johnny was snuggling his head between Estelle's legs, some poor forensic guy was probably rubbing Chinese tiger balm on his bottom lip to stop him retching from the smell of decomposing flesh.

Apparently the first policeman on the scene not only got the shock of Benny's bloated body, but found a green lizard about three feet long with a serrated collar, thick legs and long, curved claws sitting next to him. It skittered away and was later identified as an ocellated lizard –the Spanish call them lagarto ocelado, the scientists Timon Lepidus. I just call them scary. Anyway, they thought it must have come in through an open window upstairs, attracted by the smell of meat. While it usually eats only beetles, small snakes and mammals and the like, it had managed a nibble on Benny's fingers.

I still get shudders about that. Poor Benny. I really didn't know what Johnny had planned.

Naturally it was a big thing for the local constabulary. They showed it too; cars, vans, men with guns guarding each entrance to the villa, flashing lights, cordoning off everything they could think of. There was a constant parade of people up and down the same steps I had been on only a week before when Benny greeted us.

Carlos told me about that. Like I said, I didn't know him then, but later he filled me in. He'd turned up at Málaga Airport about the same time Johnny was collecting Estelle and his cash. He'd come to see Benny. He had business to do. He had made a few phone calls over the past week and couldn't get hold of Benny, not even after leaving messages. And Benny owed him five million. That's one hell of a lot of cocaine before it goes to the streets.

Now he knew why Benny didn't pick up – not just because his fingers were an amuse bouche for a lagarto ocelado, but because he was dead. He had sat outside the villa in a high-performance black Mercedes-Benz 450SEL 6.9 watching the police dance. The driver said nothing and looked straight ahead, while Carlos lowered the blackened electric windows down and stared. He could hear the electric climate control strain as the day's heat flooded the back seat and swept across his confused face. He picked up the luxury saloon's radio phone and asked the operator for a number in Italy, then tapped the driver on the shoulder. The car pulled sedately away.

I can imagine the conversation. I met the old man years later at his villa with a view, as I'd call it. Classic Italian white marble villa with views of Naples Bay. He was in a wheelchair when I met him but had a shock of healthy white hair even then. I can imagine what he'd have been like in his fifties, talking to Carlos then, people bustling about to keep him happy. Sitting on the terrace, eating, drinking, making phone calls, whispering in someone's ear. He was still doing it when I met him.

He was the 'capo in teste' from Naples. Part of the Neapolitan Camorra. And no, I'm not going to name the clan. It's more than my life's worth, even now. Besides after what I'd seen in London, Morocco, Spain, Gibraltar, I liked the Italian way of doing business, at least with this family. They at least treated me with more respect than any of the others. Although it has to be said the brutality of some of the other families was well-known too.

Yeah, the Neapolitan Camorra. It was as violent as the Sicilian Cosa Nostra. It had its own honour code like the Cosa Nostra, but it differed in one vital thing. The Camorra groups or clans acted independently of each other. There could be co-operation but there could also be conflict. That was a downside, sure, Carlos once told me, but when top members got busted or bumped off, another family would take over or a collection of clans.

Although I did know that during the late 1970s and early 80s a guy called Raffaele Cutolo formed something called Nuova Camorra Organizzata and tried to get all the families together. But it was a bit like getting the Klingons unified and failed, miserably.

Carlos's family had started off working with Turkish gangs, smuggling heroin into Northern Spain way back in the seventies. Then the gypsies would handle the retail end in Spain itself. But maybe as a result of what was going on with Cutolo in Naples, I figured that's when the family moved into Morocco and southern Spain. They dealt with the Arab gangs that ran the hash production out of bases along Jebl Mousa, which looks a little like Gibraltar. That's where they also picked up contacts with the Colombians to deal in cocaine.

To be honest me and Johnny knew all the names. We'd be over there on holiday, so to speak, loads of times. Lots would be whispered and for a reason – it meant you could avoid stepping on anyone's toes and you could go to the right person if you needed to. Me personally, I always took it to mean avoid stepping on anyone's toes and avoided going to any right person. Not that Johnny thought that way.

Yeah I can see it now. Carlos sitting with the old man on the terrace, probably drinking red wine, shaded from the bright sunlight. "Carlos are you telling me they are saying Dutch Benny died from heart failure? He was as strong as an ox, been at sea most of life and he looked after himself. No. This is not right. It stinks."

"I agree. I had Benny's boats and his house searched, along with full reports from the police. There was no sign of the merchandise or the money. That's not Benny's style."

"True. I assume you checked all of Benny's accounts?"

"Yes capo. Nothing there. His estate is being looked after by his lawyers and what's legit is legit. Benny was careful but he was also dependable," said Carlos.

"Okay I want the names of every one Benny had dealings with. You understand? Everyone. Now go see to it. And Carlos… Do not come back without a name."

I'm pretty certain the conversation went that way. Well after Benny died, it all sort of went quite for me and Johnny. He was enjoying his new villa and I was running the club. That villa of Johnny's, it was like a palace. And he'd paid for it outright and still had the luxury apartment, all paid. The boatyard outside Estepona, the club, the yard in Walworth, a couple of other London properties he was cagey about and, so I was told, a nice flat in Geneva. Yes so it all went quiet for two months it did. Nobody had come anywhere near us over Benny's death. They were still saying it was a heart attack.

But Johnny had to get back to work. Enough was never enough for Johnny, not while there was a 'mug' out there willing to be relieved of his money. And he was getting a hefty wedge from the Old Bill. The excluded what Johnny 'legitimately' sold, so to speak, to those London boys you really wanted to keep in with and right under the noses of Mr Elder & Co.

It was sometime in 1980 we took another trip to London – business was business. Anyway there was Johnny waiting for me with a Mark 2 Ford Transit. It looked like it had been pulled off a scrap heap even though it should have been a new model. I pulled the VW Camper van into the yard at Walworth Place next to him.

I must say I loved that machine, comfortable because I made sure it was stocked properly and it was a cheap, private date. I'd made a couple of trips out to the country and parked up next to a pretty country pub and enjoyed the stress-free break. I bought me own when I retired.

"Watcha' Johnny. Are we ready to rock?" I asked, trying to cheer myself up.

"Yeah. The deal is on Bill. Remember leave just two parcels in the truck," he said.

After I'd locked up the camper van and climbed into the Ford's driver's seat, next to Johnny and pulled out, I starting thinking. Then I started sniggering. By the time I had got to spluttering, Johnny finally asked me, "What's the joke, Bill? Let your old mate Johnny into it?"

"Well it's simple, I can't get my head around why people are so thick?"

That's when we both started guffawing with snot coming out my nose. How I held onto the van, I'll never know. When we stopped, Johnny turned to me and said, "Seriously what have I told you about people, Bill? Money and greed, Bill, money and greed. Put the two together and you get... what Bill, what?"

"Stupidity. Well, here we both are then, Jon," I answered, smilingly broadly.

About half an hour later we were sitting in a car park. By the time a flash Jag pulled in beside our van It was dark. "That's another reason I didn't bring the Jag tonight," said Johnny. "It loses its intended impact. This is more workman-like. Besides I don't want any mix-ups, especially with a bunch of Dirty Harrys sitting outside gagging to shoot someone."

The driver of a cherry red Jag stayed where he was but two doors opened and two men got out. The man who got out first and closest to the van was in his late twenties. He'd cropped blonde hair and had a manner that said he might be ex-army. Other than that it was blue jeans, some rock band tee shirt, baseball shoes and denim jacket. There's that bulge again, I thought, as he walked over.

The other guy looked like he was all trench coat and runners and stayed in the background, watching. His face was in the shade.

"You Mr Wilkins?" the first guy asked.

Johnny opened the van door and jumped down. He smiled. "That depends if you've got the mountain of cash I've asked you for?" He walked around to the back door of the Transit and opened it. Blondy, as I called him, followed him and peered over Johnny's shoulder. There was a lovely little packet of cocaine already split open, this time with a silver salt spoon lying across the red embossed duck.

"Ah, that's classy Mr Wilkins. I've heard a lot about you, you're a legend," said Blondy.

"Hmmm, let's cut the Eamonn Andrews 'This is Your Life' crap and stick to business. I'm a busy man but always willing to expand clientele, okay?" snapped Johnny.

Again the clientele snorted deeply, threw their head back and skyward, inhaled deeply, looked at their feet and shook their head.

"Well are you satisfied with quality?" teased Johnny.

"Ahh, yeah. I'll take all you have, as we agreed."

There's that Johnny smile again. This time he followed Blondy to the back of Jaguar and watches as Blondy lifted the already sprung boot and reached for a sports bag. One of the big ones. He opened the bag to allow Johnny to rifle through the bundled notes.

"You want to count it, Mr Wilkins?" asked Blondy.

"Like you say, son: legend. Been around a long time. So no I don't want to count it because I know where to come if it's not all there or there's any trouble, won't I, mate? Besides you've got more to come," he smiled at the end of his answer.

"Oh, of course. It's all there, mate. No problems. And, yeah, be good doing more business Mr Wilkins."

I had already unloaded two big parcels from the back of the Transit. Went back to driver's seat just as Johnny got into the van clutching the bag and stuffing it into his footwell. As we pull out, Johnny leans out his open window and waves, "be lucky, son."

We see DS Elder standing by a car, waving at Johnny to piss off.

That's when it all went wrong for Blondy. About a minute after us leaving, him and his pals took the exit to find Mr Elder standing there. He'd put that God-awful brown Granada across the road and was leaning up against it, legs crossed, smoking a fag. Big grin on his face, apparently.

By the time the boys in the Jag even considered reversing, all hell broke lose. First of all the back passenger window went through, a quick glance from the driver in the rear view mirror revealed two police men in almost-black boiler suits and blue berets pointing Enfield Enforcers fitted with a Pecar telescopic sight and screaming something, while some bloke in a leather jacket was pulling a sledge hammer from the back window. By the time he looked back in front there were two men were standing directly in front of the windscreen guns levelled, six-inch long barrels looking suitably threatening and shadows looming by each side window. Game over, man.

Son of Lucifer

Chapter Seven
Fun and Games

After Bentley and Blondy, I had a bit of a quiet life. At least I wasn't up in London with Johnny and driving around with kilos of white.

The years had passed and while I'd stayed home he had a few trips to the UK. I was never quite sure for what – possibly to off-load some more of his rather large cocaine stock, legitimately. That is to say not getting the Old Bill involved. And no doubt he did a couple of minor stings with Mr Elder, but that was to keep Mr Elder happy and his income flowing. Or at least that's what he would have said to me, had he said anything at all.

We had our little business lines together and separately. We got our fingers sticky in Gibraltar – there was always something seedy about the place and we exploited every seam of it: booze, fags, drugs, perfumes, money laundering, it was all there.

I still went on the occasional trip to Morocco with him, but it felt a little uncomfortable. He was spending a lot more time with a few Colombians who were resident looking after their interests with the Arabs, Italians and anyone else they felt like dealing with. They had a passion for heavily guarded villas with strange interpretations of pagodas, although I was told that they used them as some sort of religious altar. Like the Spanish, they had a thing about saints and Mary and statues.

In fact the Spanish and Colombians had been building up a nice little relationship since the early 80s. Former colonial master, speaking the same language had a natural attraction for the Colombian drugs lords. The only thing was a few months back two big names who'd lived in Madrid or somewhere, Jorge Luis Ochoa and Gilberto Rodríguez-Orejuela, were arrested and shipped home.

But they felt comfortable with Johnny. Plus he didn't tap them up. I had wondered if Johnny was doing big cocaine deals with them, but if he had, I'd have found out one way or another. I'm sure he had plans for them but I didn't find out until decades later exactly what. At the time I thought what plans he had didn't involve fucking them over. Although they were pretty quiet in Spain and Morocco more than at home, they could be relied on to be ruthless if you crossed them.

I figured the first of Johnny's plans was one of investment advice. Rather money laundering. Spain's banking and investment regulations could be fairly pliant, even though it was part of the European Economic Community it was, shall we say, a Latin part. Johnny was not only good with figures, although he could certainly spend it, but he also had great contacts in London, Spain, Gibraltar and Morocco.

It was in 1986 that he called the big party. I remember the "big" party. And not just for organising it for Johnny. He would show off his superb villa with eight bedrooms, triple garages, pool, Jacuzzi, private walled gardens. It was going to be at his villa and look like the United Nations.

I had to lay on Ron Medellin Añejo rum for the Colombians and Johnny demanded something called aguardiente, or guaro, made from sugar cane and flavoured with aniseed. That was twenty bottles of Antioqueño flown in. Then I had the Arab contingent, mostly Moroccans which meant someone who knew how to mix fruit juice cocktails. Also whiskey berbere – they loved their mint tea. Then there was also the real whiskey. For the Spanish, tequila and beer. For the Germans beer, mostly. I couldn't remember the rest but after getting Johnny's list of old lags who would be representing the British contingent, their selection would cover any other nationality that turned up.

I also remember it because it's when Johnny asked me to go another big job, back to London. Still that's when I was still in a party spirit. One look at Johnny's gaff proved that. I certainly had a load of cash stashed away. Here we were on the Costa del Sol, plenty of money, women and drugs. Not only that, but we were in with Her Majesty's law and we paid the Spanish police to leave us alone. From what I could see, Johnny had it figured.

I was standing in one of the small villas that walled one side of Johnny's inner yard. The cool air wafted out – these model villas had all the luxuries, aircon, bedroom with TV and sofa and en-suite. Typical Spanish style.

All around the grounds, behind palm, lemon, orange and mango trees stood groups of people. By the pool a large number of young ladies squealed wearing only bikini bottoms. They were admired by an attentive group of older men. All were drinking, especially the Moroccans.

I'd been considering an earlier event when Johnny introduced me to Juan Rodriquez who had arrived with his wife. I was told to look after him. He looked like he was in his forties but it was difficult to tell. Everything about him was perfect – his hair was in perfect place and was as dark as it could get. His hands were looked after, manicured. His English was faultless. His shirt was ironed and his silk cravat was correctly tied, his white jacket fell immaculately and the crease in his navy blue trousers was military. His manners were impeccable.

So was his wife. She had an aristocratic air and spoke English with slight accent and with a hint of disdain. I could tell she wouldn't let Juan Rodriquez stay too long, just enough to fall within good manners.

It turned out Johnny had known Juan from his time in London. From what I later learned from Johnny, ol' Juan came from both sides of the fence. His perfect manners were the result of a rather privileged childhood coming from a long line of Andalusian horse breeders, the horsey aristocracy of Spain. However at some point the family rather than the Pure Spanish Horse fell from favour.

Juan ended up studying law in London, where he honed his language skills. At some point his horsey connections kicked in and he'd got into scamming in the horse business, met Johnny and that, as they say, was that. Johnny managed to get him pupillage with a chamber of dodgy barristers that were experts on contract and commercial law with a fairly profitable criminal side thrown in.

A few years later he updated his Spanish legal qualifications at some top-notch place in Madrid and then moved back to his roots – Andalucia.

That meant him and Johnny were thick and I'd never even heard of him before. Interesting. So over to Johnny.

The waiters, all in white, were running hither and thither, as old Sid James would say. I could see Johnny by his private bar near-hidden beneath the white archway. It took me nearly five minutes to walk over to him, weaving between wavering people, along the top of the pool, avoiding the bellyflops and the ambushed divers. Then I walked around the bell tower and stepped up into the gallery room onto cool brown tiles. I remember it took my eyes a moment to adjust from the bright Andalucian light and when I saw him with the Slug, I wish I hadn't bothered with the trip.

There he was and an even bigger man now, further up the ranks, all-knowing locally and across the Costa del Sol. But still a slug.

"Listen señor Johnny, I'm enjoying this party. Don't forget that any help I can give you is… shall we say, looking after our better citizens," he laughed.

Johnny smiled his 'best friend' smile and said, "All help will be reciprocated, of course. So let me help you enjoy the party…"

He turned, saw me and winked. He glanced to one side again and beckoned to Lucy. Lucy had not exactly replaced Estelle, but she sure looked like her. Perfect body, perfect blonde hair, perfect long legs. Perfectly the Slug's cup of tea.

"Darling, stop faffing about and come here and meet someone,"Johnny said pulling her into his hips. She whimpered, "Oh Johnny not in public, please," and laughed. The contagious 'bon homee ' had obviously caught up with the Slug, whose polite smile grew into a lecherous drool.

"Now Lucy see that our chief of police has a great time while he's with us."

Not needing to be asked twice the Slug thrust his sweaty hand into Lucy's and she turned and led him into the villa.

"Nice organising, Bill. But we have some other business too, don't we?" We both filled our glasses and walked into the villa and stopped at a non-descript wooden door in a long wall. When unlocked it led to the tower, a set of stairs going up one wall. The base was windowless as was the next floor, the only light coming through cross-shaped arrow slits. This one had an office however, wooden shelves along most of three walls. There was a desk and computer and fireproof filing cabinets.

Johnny unlocked the desk drawer and pulled out a small block of white compressed powder. I watched as he cut back part of the red label with the duck on it and then scraped two lines onto a mirror on his desk.

"Well Bill how did it go with setting up the puff?" asked Johnny, who then took a deep snort of coke.

"Well all's good at the Moroccan end. We take delivery in about two weeks, date, time and place to be confirmed in seven days. But I was wondering about after we get it here, how're you getting it across to Blighty this time?" I asked.

"We'll get it back using a few bent drivers on the same ferry, preceded by a tip-off to Mr Elder. It's an oldie, but a goldy. Anyway we need to do it soon, as I'm having a few cash flow problems," confessed Johnny.

"You? Cash flow issues? I know you've been partying a bit hard but it can't be that bad, can it?" I sounded sympathetic.

"No seriously. I've got all the property but it's not exactly accessible. Plus I've been investing in a couple of deals with the Colombians," he revealed. "You remember that Brinks Mat job nearly two years ago? Well I have an 'in' with them and they're interested in swapping gold for cocaine."

Yes, the £26 million pound job at Heathrow. A heavy mob with petrol cans and lighters managed to drive away with gold, diamonds and cash. But a lot of gold.

"So I know that the gang who have it are finding it difficult to shift it," continued Johnny speaking even faster. "The Old Bill have been all over anyone in the gold trade, even coins, for the last 18 months. The Colombians, on the other hand can avoid laundering cash by getting paid in the transportable global asset of gold. And that's where I come in. Doing the organising and bringing the interested parties together and transporting gold. Nice and easy."

I looked at Johnny and refocused, "Well that doesn't make me feel so bad."

"Spit it out Bill."

"Well hearing that sob-sob story, I wasn't going to ask for any coke. I've run out, any chance? Bit of personal?" I said nodding to the packet.

"My God you don't have to ask mate. You took fuck all when we had the initial delivery. Here, finish this packet and here's a full one," he said reaching into the drawer again. "I have quite a few of those left for personal use, apart from our stash in London and at the rate you use it, you'll still have it in ten years, so I'll know where to come," he laughed.

We moved back to the party, standing at the steps overlooking the party hall. We could hear the screams and splashes from the pool, but in front of us were dancing people, champagne corks being popped, bass beat, laughing and mumbling.

Johnny stood beside me his arm over my shoulder. He burst out laughing, "Just as well I'm broke then, sorta." We both laughed.

It was nearly a month later when I met Johnny at Heathrow. It was like deja vu from six years ago. As soon as we came out of the Arrivals hall, there was DI Elder – he quickly told us that he'd been promoted – and his bloody Granada. Well it was a new 2.8 litre Mark two, but a fucking Granada nonetheless. I reckon that half the Granada's in London either were, or had been, a plain-clothes cop car. It'd got so that when I saw a Granada anywhere, I immediately thought I was being followed. I know paranoia was pretty common in our game, but when it came to that car, I began to think of it as a jinx.

Nobody said anything. Mr Elder nodded to us, and I got in the front while Johnny sat in the back. I didn't know the copper behind the wheel, no one introduced anyone and Mr Elder didn't call me Monkey MacFadden. I guessed he must be warming to me.

"Johnny, Johnny, Johnny, I appreciate the call. But seriously, how long do you really think you can get away with this particular prank? I mean it will not be long before someone catches on. Most of them are paranoid, stupid thugs, but a few are damn shrewd, with an even bigger dose of paranoia," said Mr Elder almost in a way that made you think he cared.

"What're you worried about. You're collecting bodies, ain't you?" replied Johnny in defiance. "You ain't saying you've got a soft spot for me, have you Mr Elder?"

"Listen. You keep fucking your own, my son, and I will keep locking them up. But it's you I am worried about. And Mr Farringdon wanted me to remind you that you've got other business to look after for him – the Colombians, that business in Gibraltar next year, so we do worry about you."

I was surprised to see Johnny's eyes flick up to the driver's mirror I was looking in at the mention of Mr Farringdon. "Look save it for someone who gives a fuck. You know you're getting the goods, in all sorts of ways. Just let me do what I have to and you stay on the ball."

I noticed that Mr Elder's face had mellowed over the past few years. He didn't seem to have that same incendiary-like attitude, his suits now looked like they came from John Lewis, but his eyes were as frighteningly blue as ever. He sighed, "That's all very well Johnny, but let's not forget one thing – we're still your paymasters. And it's getting bigger without you even having to leave home."

"Okay, Mr Elder I can see which way the future lies. I understand, but if you don't mind there's a couple of things about present business which need to be made clear. You'll have to be vigilant on this one coming up, as I've just found out it's part of Lenny Reed's firm." He finished the sentence and smiled at Mr Elder. Then he hesitated and looked into the mirror.

I played the game. Say nothing during negotiations or business discussions. Always be on Johnny's side. But I could feel a bead of cold sweat on my forehead, a slight nausea in the belly and my arsehole tightening. It really does you know.

This time it was DI Elder's turn to smile, "Now you see why we're concerned, Johnny. Lenny Reed's firm is a nasty bunch of animals. You getting cold feet after all?"

"No, not at all. You know me Mr Elder, I like to dot all the 'i's and cross the 't's. I have it figured but I just don't want to end up dead for the lack of any coppers showing up and tooled up."

Mr Elder had stopped smiling by now and glanced out the side window at the taxis pulling past. It was only then I noticed there was motorbike cop sitting on the other side of the road at the end of the car park, just sitting, just watching. "Well Johnny what're you dealing with this time? Coke? It'd be nice to take Lenny Reed out of his game. Or at least off his game. Although he has his uses."

Johnny's eyes flicked to look at Mr Elder when he heard the last comment and without a break answered, "Nah, nothing that big. Just about a hundred kay of blow, Moroccan resin."

Mr Elder raised his eyebrows. "That's a bit small-fry for Lenny. New horizons, eh, son? You just make sure I get bodies on the day. No fuck ups. Alright. Johnny stay in touch. Bill look after him," he looked into my eyes in the mirror. It was the first time he ever called me Bill. Another one of those times when you really wish that you'd listened to your gut.

It was only the next day that the subject of Lenny came up between me and Johnny. We'd picked up the VW Camper van from Walworth and were heading for the meet. Yeah I didn't understand why Johnny wanted to use it either. But the old Jag wasn't around any more. It disappeared during one of Johnny's visits to London a couple of years ago. Like I said, he kept stuff to himself.

"Look Johnny I don't understand why we're using the VW Camper van. It's not only got all the dope it's also got most of our remaining coke, seems a bit risky," I ventured, quietly.

"Look, this should be a breeze Bill, in and out mate. Besides where's safer for the gear than with a bunch of armed coppers looking after it? And protection."

I glanced over from above the VW Camper van steering wheel and looked into Johnny's eyes, "Yeah, but this deal ain't with two bob drug dealers though is it?"

He glared at me, "What are you saying Bill?"

"Well, I was just saying. This is not run-of-the-mill druggies we are about to rip off is it? There could be serious ramifications on this one and even Joe Wilkins' reputation might not see off Lenny," I glanced back to the road and waited.

"The problem you have Bill, and is where you are, is that you have no vision… Not to mention bottle."

I sighed, "Doing business with the Arabs or some of the firms is one thing but I don't mind saying my bottle's gone when dealing with Lenny Reed, mate. You know how he works, he's an animal. People go missing with him, mate. It's not worth the hassle-factor."

Then Johnny started laughing. "Don't. Don't. You're scaring me. Remember I kept my Soho businesses when the Krays and the Richardsons were at war. Don't you think I ain't worked out Len Reed. Yeah, he's an animal, but only if he knows we have fucked his boys, yeah?" He looked out the window and said firmly, "We go in."

Neither of us spoke for a couple of minutes.

In a more conciliatory tone Johnny continued. "As far as Len knows, the deal was done, we had left and are in the clear and Elder then nicks his boys."

"But what about the quantity of puff Johnny?"

"Look it's not as if we haven't done this before is it? Like I said, Len's not an idiot. He knows the Old Bill take a lump out of the load, or it goes missing somewhere along the route. As for D S Elder, he ain't about to blow the whistle on the amount. All he's interested in is bodies," he replied confidently.

"Well I would not like to be in your shoes if Reed did find out."

"Now Bill, you mean 'us' don't you? Don't worry mate. It's all in hand. We drop the two large boxes I packed and keep the rest in the compartment. Bollocks to 'em!"

That put an end to that conversation. But it didn't stop me from worrying. I really wanted to be back in Spain.

It didn't take much longer to reach our destination, a warehouse of a hanger proportions. In those days most of the south bank remained undeveloped: no Tate Modern. No Globe Theatre. No modern Financial Times office. No new London Council building. Many riverside industrial buildings had yet to be converted into luxury flats, some still remained boarded off with holes from the Second World War still unfixed. Red brick in the maze of roads and allyways around the Southwark Bridge Road, you could always find a discrete warehouse. And Lenny would know who to talk to and who to bribe.

Johnny gave me directions, left, right, right. I didn't know which street I was in, I was just concentrating on avoiding meandering pedestrians. And bloody motorcycle couriers. This wasn't the best area for navigating a lumpy VW. Oh for the Jag.

At Johnny's behest, I drove into a darkened warehouse through open double doors and turned to face outwards. I personally wanted out of here as fast as possible.

We sat there for about five minutes. Silently, except for Johnny quietly humming to himself every now and again. It came something as a relief to see a blue Volvo estate pull in through the double doors and pull around to the back of the camper van. Before it had pulled up we had jumped down and went around to the back to open

That's when things got hazy. Well some things just went over my head, while at the same time I was noticing odd things. On the back window of the Volvo was a 'Baby on board' sticker. Really?

That's when I met Alfie. He got out of the passenger door and walked towards us. He was about five foot eight high but solid. He looked sallow, a dark mid-morning growth reflecting his dark lanky hair. He was dressed in black too. Black polo neck, black waist-length leather jacket. Black Levi jeans, black brogues.

Then he reached around the back of his jacket and pulled out a shooter. A fucking big one, complete with silencer. Johnny later told me it was a .357 IMI Desert Eagle, one of the few semi-automatic pistols that fire the .357 Magnum cartridge.

I couldn't care less what fucking make it was. It was pointing at me. "On the floor. On the floor. Now. If I see any movement you're fucking dead... You hear me? Dead," Alfie said in a clear, calm and precise way. I later found out that Alfie was one of Lenny Reed's nutters. Apart from having a genuine affection for firearms he had a streak of grade A nastiness all the way down his back to his bum hole. His hobby was going to the dog fights down around the Aylesbury Estate and in Peckham. I think they're barbaric and even Johnny couldn't drag me to one of those.

By the time he'd finished the sentence I'd already hit

the dusty concrete floor. I could hear Johnny dropping next to me, looking at me an expression that said, "This is not meant to happen."

But I was thinking of the Volvo's driver I'd seen through the wind shield as I was dropping. One of those slow-motion glances as I tried to avoid eye contact with Alfie or his gun that just stuck in my head. Fuck that guy looks like Johnny. Same haircut, same colour hair. Those dreadful sideburns. The Michael Caine glasses. He looked like he'd be Johnny's six foot three height too.

The Johnny spoke. "What is going on? What is this? Do you know who you're dealing with?"

I could hear Alfie poking around in the back of the camper. He found the two larger boxes we were about to give him. Some of it was real, some of it wasn't. It was the way it was packed. But it seemed Alfie was smarter than the gun gave him credit. He obviously found the, er, bad stuff.

"Shit! You'd try to serve me this shit? You fucking cheating cunts. I should shoot you right now," he said in an absurdly calm voice. Neither me nor Johnny moved or spoke or breathed. I could him pulling at things in the camper van, things being thrown, a muffled profanity. Then I heard him clearly as he leaned back out of the side door and repeated, "Don't move a fucking muscle."

He must have found the secret compartment. Maybe it wasn't that secret anyway. "This is more like it. A lovely bit of smoke to be washed down with a good snort of the marching powder," said Alfie. He repeated again as he got out of the VW and shut the door.

I didn't see him but he must have gestured to the driver in the Volvo. I heard the car door open and Alfie repeated what he said, more clearly and added, "C'mon pal get behind the wheel of the camper and pull your collar up. Hurry up… Quickly."

It was then I broke our Trappist vow and whispered to Johnny, "They're going to kill us…"

Johnny was furious and snarled, "Shut your mouth."

Then I heard Alfie standing right behind me. The hairs on the back of my neck went up. "No, not today lads. Not today. Stay lucky," laughed Alfie.

I heard the back door of the VW slam closed, then the passenger door. Next thing I knew the engine throbbed to life, there's a screech of tyres, a choking blast of exhaust fumes and our living drove off into the distance.

Last thing I heard through the open passenger window was Alfie telling the driver not to drive too fast.

By the time I'd decided to get to my feet. Johnny was already standing by the Volvo kicking shit out of the passenger side door. I was brushing down the dust, not daring to say anything, trying to look at the arse of my pants to make sure I hadn't shit myself at some point in the previous five minutes.

Then two police cars came screaming into the warehouse, one driving right, the other left, windows down, some bloody screaming, but I can't make it out. Then in comes a blue British Gas Corporation van followed by a fucking Granada. Suddenly all I could think of was which was worse – still using the Granada or still using the blue British Gas Corporation van? Especially since Mrs Thatcher had just privatised it. Suppose budgets were tight.

Shouts of "Police". "Stand where you are." "Hands up" even a couple of "Freezes" came from every direction. I obliged, but Johnny kept kicking the Volvo.

After D S Elder got out of his car, hands outstretched, shouting "Stand down, they're ours," he turned to Johnny and walked up to him.

"Okay, what the fuck happened here then? Why are you still here and where are the other two? I'm supposing I'm not going to like the answer, am I Joe?"

I didn't say anything. I was too concerned with the confused looks on the police marksmen. It looked like a recipe for a shooting.

"They fucking turned me over... Took the lot. Puff and cash and my fucking van. Where were you?" asked Johnny accusingly.

I thought Mr Elder was going to have a coronary. His face was changing colour. He looked like he was holding his breath. He certainly had his fists clenched. He turned around and shouted in rage. "All right you lot clear the area. Everybody out now."

There were a couple of minutes of activity and noise.

Mr Elder said nothing, looked at his shoes and had his hands on hips. "What a fuck up. One almighty fuck up. And I blame you, Mr Wilkins."

Johnny looked defiant. He wasn't smiling now. His face was almost contorted, "What do you mean, me? You just let them drive straight past you and your men."

"Only because I thought it was you going past me. That's the signal right? You come out; I go in, or did you decide to change it without telling me?"

"Well what the fuck did you expect me to do with a shooter pointed at me head. I couldn't get to a phone could I?" said Johnny getting his control back.

Mr Elder just looked around the warehouse. Nothing except the three of them, the Volvo and plumes of dust illuminated by shafts of light through the roof. No bodies, literally and metaphorically. The he looked back at both of us.

"I should be fucking nicking you, you bastard," he shouted.

A Johnny in control can be an artist to behold. He mimicked Mr Elder's sweep of the room. "I'd like to see that Mr Elder. I mean, what for? Loitering with intent? Listen to yourself. They had to know. Someone tipped them off." Then he turned to me, "That's why they never shot us Bill. They knew him and his men…" he nodded to Mr Elder, "were outside waiting."

I'd had enough. "Fuck all of this. I'm going home to Spain. It's quieter. Better class of people."

Elder seemed to have cooled down because he said, "That ain't a bad idea. Get going while I try to sort something out of this mess."

When we came out of the warehouse, the van had gone but there more uniforms and the plain clothes coppers remained. Elder walked ahead of us and barked a curt order to a uniformed sergeant, "Get the forensic boys down here and check that motor out. Strip it, if needs be. The rest of you meet back at the station for debriefing."

Me and Johnny just kind of wandered off, rounded a corner, flagged down a black cab and headed back to the hotel. I leaned over told the driver where to go, then pulled the glass window closed. "I don't like this. If they knew what we were planning, why let us walk away. They're not going to let us."

"Relax, Bill. Firstly they couldn't do nothing in the warehouse because of all the Old Bill parked outside. Let's just get home."

"Yeah and we still have to pay for the puff we've lost today, plus all that coke, that's a bastard," I said without thinking. I could feel the air change, crackle, smell dirty and bitter. Johnny was staring at me with hate in his eyes. That was the first time I was the one face-to-face with the Lucifer look.

Right then I felt scared. I felt scared of Johnny, I felt scared of Lenny. Forgetting and forgiving weren't Lenny's trademarks.

Chapter Eight
Rumbled

Several weeks before Bill and Johnny's bad day Lenny Reed had been looking at his drink, revolving the glass with his fingers, the golden liquor slopping around the rim. He had thin fingers, almost elegant but certainly not effete. Least-ways not that you'd say.

The night club wasn't busy. It was mid-week but it was a good place to do business at least sometimes, dark with private cubicles, legal heavies and plenty of booze and girls.

Lenny was known amongst his contemporaries as being volatile. Hovering around forty years old, Lenny's look matched his reputation. Just under six foot, he was heavy-set with big hands, just right to get around a man's throat. His full face was framed by well-kept short brown hair.

Sitting opposite him was a much slimmer man with wispy blond hair. Dave didn't want to interrupt Lenny's meditation. Lenny was, as Dave would describe it, 'touchy'. You were never quite sure what was going through his head, whether he blamed you for whatever bad news you presented or whether he forgot you were there and was venting his wrath at the news itself. There were signs – hours of abject silence, regular intake of cocaine, pie and mash sold out and business issues, but still you never quite knew.

Dave was about 30 and had worked for Lenny for just over ten years. He was used to doing the running around for him and was just back from West Yorkshire with news for Lenny. He looked around the club, thinking it could do with a bit of a spruce up. Mind you, it was a damn site more attractive than where he'd spent the last few days.

Lenny had sent him to Her Majesty's Prison Wakefield. Category A. Also known as Monster Mansion because there were murderers, drug dealers but primarily because there were so many sex offenders. Every perversion that could be thought of had been practised by these people. It was sort of a business-cum-social engagement for Dave. Lenny had a few people at Wakefield that he wanted to check on. Some of them had already kept stum during trials or were owed by Lenny. Others just needed to be reminded that Lenny was still thinking of them.

The minutes had passed so Dave let out a sigh and tried again. "I'm telling you, Len. When I was up at Wakefield I also saw Bentley. I know his gang have been paying you back the money he owes you, but he had something else to tell me. He confirmed it to me."

He described how Bentley had sat opposite Dave with his hands crossed leaning on the Formica table. "Here's the guy now," Bentley had said, his eyes moving across the room to the doorway. A man with cropped blonde hair and an upright posture nodded to Bentley then moved across to a table with a young healthy looking brunette sitting looking at him.

Dave had watched Blondy sit down with his wife and turned back to Bentley. "Yeah that's him. He came up to me on the wing and asked if I knew Joe Wilkins. I was cagey but he said he was done immediately after he did a deal with him. The Old Bill came screaming into the car park all tooled up. He said he hadn't thought much about it at the time and thought that he'd been followed. Well then he got to hear about me and my deal with Joe. He only got transferred here two weeks ago," Bentley had whispered.

Lenny had remained staring at his glass but Dave could see he was listening. "So what you're saying to me is Joe Wilkins set the deal up with the coke that Bentley got nicked for? And this Blondy bloke?" asked Lenny.

"That's what I'm saying. I did a bit of asking around when I got back and found that the Blondy story holds up. He's ex-army, had been a Lieutenant in the Blues and Royals. After he got out, he used contacts he had in the City and supplied coke exclusively to the banker brigade, he did a deal with Joe and immediately got busted," explained Dave. "It's down to Joe Wilkins that Bentley got busted."

"Listen to me, Dave, you have to be exact in your information about someone before you can say he is a grass, especially someone with the reputation of Joe Wilkins," warned Lenny.

"I know, I know, but don't you think it a little bit of a coincidence that Bentley and this other guy gets nicked in exactly the same way?"

"When is that shipment of blow coming in to us and what's it costing? Alfie's running it, ain't he?" asked Lenny.

"Yeah it's Alfie's deal and it's next week for half a million pounds," answered Dave.

"And that's been set up with Wilkins ain't it? Well leave it with me… And Dave. Not a word of this to anyone. Right?"

The day before Alfie was set to meet Joe, Dave and Lenny had another meeting. Lenny had made a decision. Not that Dave didn't already know what that decision would be. Well at least cruelty would be involved. This time Dave met Lenny in his office. Lenny really preferred his office. It might have been above his bookies but it didn't look it. He'd had some rooms knocked together and bought oak panelling for the lower walls from an architectural scrap yard. The fireplace had been 'upgraded' too.

There was a desk to one side, behind it a book-lined wall. Apart from two leather sofas and a full-sized billiard table, there were other accoutrements of a Victorian study.

They were sitting in brown button-backed leather armchairs holding cut Waterford Crystal whiskey glasses and swilling the contents gently. "Now Dave next we meet, it'll be sending Alfie off for the deal. But you gotta do something before then but it's important. Get one of our lads who looks a bit like Joe Wilkins, you know six three. If he hasn't got the same hairstyle, send him to the saloon or get him a wig. He has to be a ringer from twenty feet anyway. Don't forget sunglasses or normal glasses. You know what I mean," he said in a quiet voice.

"Yeah alright Len. No problem, mate, I've got the very bloke in mind. I'll bring him to the meet all geared up. You got a plan then Len?" asked Dave.

"I always have a plan, Dave. I always have a plan," but he was interrupted by the phone ringing on his desk. "In fact," he said as he left the armchair and walked over to his desk to pick up the phone, "This is probably part of it now."

"Hello, Lenny here… Ah yeah been expecting this call. So did your man do the job I asked for?"

Dave could make out the voice at the other end. "Well Len you were spot on. Just as well we picked them up at the airport. All over him they are mate. If I were you, I would swallow this meet. Just don't deal with him."

Lenny turned to face Dave and smiled. "Oh no, I have a little surprise for our mate Lucifer and it's time someone gave him some of his own medicine. The bastard. Cheers mate." He put the phone down and returned to his chair.

"Next time we meet Dave have that look-alike ready and tell Alfie not to worry. I'll give you the full SP then. But don't worry about the Old Bill either."

Just about the time Johnny was telling Bill that he'd no vision… not to mention bottle, four men walked down to a blue Volvo Estate. Joe's ringer was carrying a plumber's canvas bag. He opened the rear door and put the bag in the back seat within reach of the driver's seat, flicking it open to make sure the sawn-off double-barrel shotgun hadn't mysteriously walked off at some point. He then stood at the driver's door and looked at Dave and Lenny.

Alfie stood by the passenger side door, also looking at Lenny. "Okay when you go in there do it fast and do it quietly. Keep your heads down," counselled Lenny.

Dave looked him now, "You sure this is going to go our way, Len?"

He ignored the comment. "Don't look so worried Alfie. I said keep your heads down. It'll be swarming with Old Bill, but that won't happen if you do exactly what I told you," said Lenny, getting slightly annoyed.

Alfie looked quizzically at Dave and asked, "Which Old Bill is this then? We just go in and get nicked?"

It was too much for Lenny. He turned to Dave and shouted, "I thought you explained to these fucking idiots what's going on?"

It was Dave's turn to feel a little concerned. A bad-tempered Lenny on a job was not something you wanted to witness let alone be on the receiving end. "Fuck sake Alfie, how many times did I tell you about the scam. Just do as you have been told."

That seemed to satisfy Alfie for a moment. But then he turned back to Lenny and asked, "I know about the blow but what about the money?"

Dave waited for another explosion. But this time Lenny slapped his hand to his head and rolled his eyes heavenward. "For Christ's sake Alf. Just go and don't forget the radio."

As Alfie and Joe Number Two prepared to leave, Lenny leant down and said, "Fasten your seat belts boys. You don't want to get nicked, do you?" He turned to Dave. "Alright gimme the radio. Let's find out what's going on."

"This Mobile Green dispatch centre, to Mobile Green One. Over."

"Yeah I'm here. Over."

"Alright mate? What's happening there? Over."

Just along the street from the Southwark meet, while Bill and Johnny sit waiting in the musty warehouse, there was a man leaning against a motorcycle in full dispatch rider gear. The bike had a flat tyre, but the man is more intent on an earpiece attached to his walkie-talkie. "Well," he crouched down to look at the wheel rim more closely. "I can see a couple of cars down one end the street and a blue British Gas Corporation van down the other end. Hang on, there's a Granada pulling up next to the van… It's DI Elder, like you thought. Yep that's mister Elder okay. Okay, so that's three cars and one van that I can see. There might be one around the corner down the other end. But if there's that many they're definitely tooled up. Over."

"You sure it's him, mate? Over."

"Nah, no doubt. It's DI Elder. He's back in his

motor and moving off. Listen Joe Wilkins has already turned up he's waiting. Over."

"Excellent. Mobile Green dispatch centre, to Mobile Green Two, over."

Dave listened to static. Lenny sighed. "Alfie, wake up you dopey fuck."

"Er sorry boss. Over. We're just going into the warehouse now, over and out," said Alfie. He turned to Joe Number Two and said, "Just wait in the car and keep the shotgun low."

"Okay Mobile Green dispatch centre, to Mobile Green One, keep an eye on the gates and as soon as a VW camper van comes out, clear off sharpish. Over," crackled Lenny.

"Roger, see you back at base over and out," said the motorbike courier. He attached a foot pump and began getting the tyre up and running. He had just managed to tighten the cap on the air nozzle, when the VW turned out of the warehouse gates and left in the opposite direction. As the motor courier powered away two cars passed him and turned towards the warehouse.

Ten minutes later he joined Lenny, Dave, Alfie and Joe Number Two in the office. Some had whiskey in the crystal set, others were swigging lager from the neck. They were all standing looking at a pallet with blocks and blocks of Morroccan puff. "Lovely, jubley," sniggered Lenny. "Quality Moroccan hashish from the central Rif or the west and southern provinces including Chefchaouen, Larache and Taounate. Only the best for

our Joe. And look at this amusing amount of Coke."
He picked up one of the bags of cocaine, running his
fingers over the embossed red duck, and looking at the
smaller labels through the opaque wrapping. "That's
how you fuck grasses at their own game."

"But Lenny why didn't we kill the bastards then?"
asked Dave.

"With all those coppers ready for a rumble and
tooled up and you want to pop him. Are you mad? No,
for Joe fucking Wilkins losing half a million quid will
hurt him much more, than legs. At least for the minute.
Let's see how he likes it done to him."

Chapter Nine
Paying for the Puff

I don't mind telling you, I shat myself all the way back to Spain. Even then I kept looking out for Lenny. I was running the club and had avoided Johnny's company for the past two weeks. I knew he was brooding in that huge villa. It was pointless stating the obvious again and he won't be too happy that I'd warned him. Nah, better to make myself scarce, couple of trips to Gib. That sort of thing. He'd be racking his brains on how to get back on top.

But that strategy was forced to an abrupt end when Saeed turned up at the bar of the club one afternoon. He didn't look too pleased, but I explained I hadn't seen Johnny for nearly two weeks. He said Johnny was late with his payment and he would meet me at the club and then we'd both to Johnny's villa tonight at seven. That was that.

I really didn't want to mess with Saeed. Apart from the fact his own family were bad enough, he also had friends. I knew he was linked to the family of Abdelaziz El Yakhloufi, they did business. Then on top of that they employed a lot of people in Morocco, and doing good for a discontented poor who had no channels of representation meant they had a lot of muscle.

I just agreed and called Johnny to tell him what was happening whether he liked it or not. Saeed was not for delaying payment.

It reminded me of the evening with Benny. But this time it was the opposite way around. Saeed was a big man, about six foot five inches. He was broad too. He had a farmer's hands – he must a done a fair bit of planting himself, I thought. He was about 35, typical Moroccan-brown complexion and short cropped hair. He was dressed better than Benny too, even though the suit was beige and so were the shoes. We'd driven into Johnny's front courtyard and walked up the marble steps to the heavy oak wooden double doors.

Johnny swung one door open with a drink in his hand. It looked like rum. There was that big smile. "Saeed, welcome, my friend and Bill, it's been too long," he said as he lead us down another three steps to his living room. This breezy 'bon homie' stank. Johnny was up to something. I hope he didn't think he had an angle, from Saeed's silence all the way over in the car, I didn't think he'd go for it.

He stood over by the elaborate antique marble-manteled fireplace, next to a small fire burning in the wrought iron grate. "I like the watching the flames, even though it's baking," said Johnny. He motioned for Saeed to sit on the sofa. I decided on the armchair.

"Drink, Saeed? Bill get the man a drink," he offered. "What brings you over? I could have picked you and got you here quicker, you know that. Look my friend if you're here about the money for the gear, you know I'm good for it! Always have been."

Then Saeed spoke. He chose his words carefully and slowly. "Look Johnny, I served you in good faith. The

Son of Lucifer

money is already a week overdue. I thought you might have at least contacted me. Where is my money?"

"Yeah, well I'm sorry about that. Listen, I'll be straight, due to unforeseen circumstances at the other end, I've now got a cash flow problem. However do not despair I have got twenty grand for you to be going on with," said Johnny. He eyes flicked to look at mine. I didn't think this was going to work.

"C'mon we've done business for years. Cut me some slack…"

Saeed cut across Johnny's plea. "That's no good Johnny. You have already used your good will with me. I pulled this together for you and my people will want to know where the cash is. At the moment you're in no danger since they know nothing about it. But at the end of the month everything will be pulled together."

"Oh so you're telling me you've been giving me credit without the rest of the family knowing?" said Johnny suddenly alert.

"I will not go back without my two hundred and fifty thousand pounds," he said determinedly and looking straight at Johnny.

"Oh shit mate. I'm fucking glad you told me. Like I said, we're mates… hang on… Just wait there… I'll get the rest for you. I didn't how much shit you personally would be in," said Johnny apologetically as he moved away from the fireplace. He looked at me smiling and winked. He then crossed the room, up the marble steps past the dining room table and into the kitchen.

"I'm sorry about all this Saeed," I said.

"At least we can resolve it, amicably and now," Saeed said, less business-like. "Maybe I'll have that drink, Bill, make it whiskey."

As I turned to go to the drinks cabinet in the corner, the free-standing globe already opened, I could hear Johnny clattering along the tiles to come back to the dining room. "Ice?" I asked Saeed.

"Yes please, two cubes and make it Irish, Bill."

By the time I had plonked the ice in his glass and gently poured a good shot of Jameson's into his glass, Johnny was standing by in front of Saeed holding out an expensive Spanish leather travel bag with his left hand, dropping it at Saeed's feet.

"It's all there mate, just check it… a cool quarter of a million," Johnny cajoled.

It was then as Saeed leaned forward, head down to reach and open the straps, I noticed what was in Johnny's right hand held straight down by the side of his leg. He brought the carving knife up and straight through Saeed's back into his heart. Johnny knew all about how to cut someone, maybe as punishment or as a warning. Or, in this case, to kill you.

The knife jutted out of his back and blood only oozed. Saeed suddenly reared backwards, head up gasping for air. Johnny moved back, as Saeed's right arm tried to reach behind him and find the knife. The flailing lasted only a few seconds.

I stopped looking. "Oh fuck, Johnny what have you done now? You know what Saeed's family are like and the people they do business with," I squealed. I just looked and looked. It was real. There was a dead body sitting on the sofa. I had seen Johnny with the Moroccan perfume bottle at Benny's. We hadn't discussed Benny's death except when I first told Johnny. Then he didn't say much except,"Shame" and "Nice bloke", that sort thing. I had my suspicions but now I knew. Benny and heart attack, phaw! Benny trusted Johnny that's what happened.

By now Johnny was rummaging in beige pockets. He pulled out a wallet, extracted one hundred and sixty thousand pesatas and one hundred thousand dirhams. He tossed the wallet onto Saeed's chest.

"Seriously Johnny what the fuck is going through your mind," I asked again.

"You heard him. No one else knew he had done the deal with us, so we're clear on the motive front, calm down, Bill."

I had calmed down a little by then. "Look you have killed him, murdered him, stabbed him etcetera. I don't want to get mixed up in murder, Johnny. And what about cleaning up this mess?"

"I'll have Pedro take care of the floor and sofa. Tell him it was punch-up between some old lags from home over football, he'll believe that. It's easy – cold water first, then a bleach mix, then hot water with detergent. You and me will take care of Saeed," Johnny paused and pulled the knife out of the dead man's back. He slowly and deliberately wiped the blade on Saeed's suit.

That's when it got worse. He turned to me pointing the blade at my face. He spoke quietly. "Who called me to tell me Saeed had arrived to see me? And who was it that brought him here, you idiot? And about murder: what about Benny? It's all the same. Listen…" Johnny stopped talking then. He lowered the knife, looked into my eyes and said, "If I didn't know any better, I could start to think you're not to be trusted."

Deep down I knew he was right. I didn't have any choice right now. He'd confirmed what he'd done to Benny. I'd liked Benny. Now it was Saeed. That's forgetting fucking the Lenny Reed nightmare.

"Okay so what we going to do with him? Can't have Pedro cleaning up around him," trying the light-hearted approach.

Johnny smiled again, "That's better, Bill. Now help me wrap him up ready for the boat tomorrow morning. We'll have a few drinks and leave just before sunrise. We'll pop him in the boot of the Range Rover take him down to the boat shed, take out a SeaRider, a few chains and 'bosh' no Saeed, problem solved. Right?"

He handed me half the currency he'd taken from Saeed's wallet. Oh fuck I'm up to my neck in shit now. Now I could understand why some called him Lucifer.

Saeed had trusted Johnny. Bad idea.

Chapter Ten
The Bad Pants Day

Of course that wasn't the last we heard of Saeed. We'd both worked that out. Now it was to play on absence of motive, good relations and being a source. Some two weeks later Johnny called me to say I had to join him. Saeed's family had been asking questions. I'd been asked to meet with Saeed's brother and business partner.

I was beginning to dread this two week time cycle. I wanted to go back to my relatively stress free lifestyle. A bit of ducking and diving but no-one after me. No big deals, peace and quiet.

It was an uneventful drive up to Gibraltar. Me and Johnny didn't talk that much but he seemed cheerful enough. He told me not worry besides he had something else coming up. We pulled the Range Rover into a space along Line Wall Road and walked back to Casement Square.

I like the thoughts of such a public place. Better than some fucking warehouse. On the other hand – and not that I'm superstitious, but I knew about Casemates Square.

Sure now it was Casemates Square, a "celebration of peace" according to the tourist marketing. You know, a place for people of different beliefs and ethnic backgrounds. Glass-blowing, art, restaurants, cafes, yogurt-weaving. The enclosed space was surrounded by walls accessed through arches cut in them and grand grey buildings. A nineteenth century barracks was to the north of the square. Even into the 20th century it was also used for public hangings. I didn't mention it to Johnny.

We could see Saeed's brother, Youssef, sitting across the square at an outside table of some place called The Tunnel. "Remember, leave the talking to me, Bill, as usual," muttered Johnny.

"Alright but what if they ask me if I had seen him?"

"Look, just tell them the truth – everything up to coming to me…"

And that was the first time I met Carlos. He was in his 30s and looked every part the person he was. Dark hair, cut short and immaculate. Manicured fingers. Neapolitan nose. He was a good-looking lad and had the Italian taste for style. He wore an open-necked white shirt – Versace. Expensive looking off-white trousers and what looked like a good pair of brown English hand-made brogues.

He took his sunglasses off as he stood to be introduced to us both by Youssef. Youssef was not much like his brother, slim, shorter and younger but self-assured, nonetheless.

Now I know Johnny doesn't like what he doesn't know. While we went through the social palaver of ordering tea, Johnny said nothing and stared at Carlos.

Carlos ignored the look and continued with polite niceties while we waited for the order to arrive.

As the waiter turned from leaving the tea, Youssef leaned forward, speaking softly. "Johnny I've asked you to meet with me because we have some concerns. As I said this is Carlos and he represents an Italian investor in our business. This, he felt, also concerned him and I concur. This problem…"

"Problem? What Problem?" interrupted Johnny. Carlos looked more intently at Johnny then, not that Johnny noticed.

"When did you last see Saeed?" asked Youssef.

It was then Johnny seemed to get animated. "This is about Saeed. Here, now. I hope there is no funny business here. I saw him about two weeks ago as I had a little private business with him. He owed me a little cash. He coughed up, had a whiskey and fucked off. Isn't that right Bill?"

Fuck you Johnny, I thought. Why drag me into it, you wanker?

"Yeah. He just turned up at the club, we had a chat made some arrangements and I took him to Johnny's villa," I said truthfully. Even though it was true I got a certain feeling that Carlos, at least, smelled a rat.

"Look we've know each other for years Youssef, why can't you tell me what's up," Johnny pushed.

"What happened after he gave you money?"

"Well Bill left, me and Saeed a couple of

whiskeys, he asked if I knew any good bars for the birds, the usual. Filthy bastard," Johnny sniggered.

And that's when Carlos spoke on the subject. It was a cold, factual statement with a dripping warning. "Well, he never showed at his hotel that night or called in, which is very unusual wouldn't you say?"

Lucifer locked eyes with Carlos and dropped his tone of voice. "Now listen Carlos, Saeed is over 21. He can do as he pleases, but if you have anything else to say spit it out. If not, meeting's over."

Johnny got up determinedly from the table. "C'mon Bill, let's go home. Youssef if I see Saeed or hear from him, I'll call you. Enjoy your trip back to Italy, Carlos."

As we walked across the square I could feel both their eyes following us, looking for any chink in our armour. I was feeling sick.

That was another case of learning what was happening while you were doing something else.

As we walked towards an archway, I asked Johnny, "What do you think? Do you think they know something?"

Over at the table, Carlos told Youssef, "I don't like this Johnny person. He's lying, I can feel it".

Then Johnny surprised me by saying, "I think we will have to leave the drug game alone for a bit Bill. That's what I think. Did you see how that Italian was looking at me?"

He continued, "Don't worry these guys know they

have to have proof, especially with us and they ain't got nothing. We're away scot-free mate."

I guess that's when Youssef leaned into Carlos and, "Oh a liar he is my Italian friend but do you know why? Carlos, my brother was, how you call it in Europe – gay. The last thing he would ask is about is women. Booze, gambling maybe, but not women."

I still think about that day. It was when I should have packed my bags and headed off to my nice little all-paid bolt-hole that no one, including Johnny knew about. But I'll keep that to myself, as it still could have its uses.

I did not like the way Carlos or Youssef had looked at Johnny. I think he'd wound them up on top of everything. But I also knew, like Johnny, that if you became too co-operative or apologetic that smacked of weakness. If we were innocent Johnny would have reacted the same way.

We took our time getting back to Estepona, I guess we'd used more adrenalin at the morning meeting than we'd expected. As with so many other journeys, Johnny had sunk into quiet contemplation. You could almost hear cogs whirring. As we entered Estepona, he perked up a little. "Bollocks mate, it's been a heavy day so far. But the sun's still there, how 'bout we sit by the pool, chat and have a few quiet beers. I have a little surprise that might cheer you up."

"Sure Johnny, that sounds like a good idea. I need some time out after that crap."

I pulled into the short avenue of palm trees. The

metal gates lay open and I pulled the car in left to leave beside the garages' parking area. "Thank fuck we're home. Beer time," said Johnny. "Amen to that," I laughed.

I stopped pretty quick. As we stepped out of the car I was confronted by someone I didn't know but he was holding a baseball bat. That was a bad sign. I looked over to Johnny who was facing two others. "Oh fuck," I thought. "That's Lenny Reed and Alfie. We've had it now."

Alfie looked as dark in the Spanish sun as he had in that warehouse in Southwark. He was still dressed all in black. His hair looked no better. Except in place of a pistol he was holding a club hammer. I'd say it was a four pound Spear and Jackson. That meant he brought it with him. Double oh fuck.

I thought I'd make a dash up through the arches and head to one of the small villas that walled one side of the back courtyard. I kept a gun there. I didn't make it far. I found out later that it was Dave who brought me down with a swing to my leg. I went down. I didn't know what happened next except that it involved bad bruising. Dave dragged me by the back of my jacket round to the back of the Range Rover.

Johnny was already pinned against the back of the Range Rover. I found myself looking at his blue canvas sailing shoes. "Did you really think I had forgotten you… Grass!" Lenny didn't so much shout it, as snarl it. I could feel drops of spit on my bloodied face.

I think Johnny had resigned himself that it was all over. His voice didn't falter. It wasn't threatening, but it wasn't submissive. It was as if the consequences were immaterial, "Is there anything I can say to make this better for you Lenny? Money?"

All the attention was now focused on Johnny. I could see Alfie swinging the hammer in his face. Lenny was reaching for something in his pocket. Johnny was just looking at him. It's funny how your mind finds a microsecond an eternity to remember and reason and clarify. I knew why Johnny didn't have a bead of sweat on his face while Lenny swore and ranted in his face. His missus had once told me the story at one of Johnny, or Joe's as it was then, nightclub. Winston's I think. Pearl said that was 1972 and she was meeting Joe at his office above another club. They were going out to some big champagne bash Joe had organised. Pearl said she was in a silver gown and all the jewels Joe had bought her. Worth a pretty penny.

As she got to the office door she heard three bangs. No words. No cries. Four men opened the door and brushed past her in the corridor, hats pulled low heavy coat collars pulled high. They continued walking unhurriedly away. She said she found Joe behind his desk lying on the floor. There was blood gushing from his shoulder and chest. She said she just screamed for help, thinking he was dead. It turned out he'd only been hit twice. Part of a turf war was all Joe would ever say about it.

"Try to rob me and have my boys nicked as well?

You slag! We're going to fix things slowly," screamed Lenny. By now I could see a little clearer and Lenny's face was almost purple, veins throbbing in the back of his hands on his neck. There was some quick movement I couldn't make out.

Lenny had moved to Johnny's side and put a plastic bag over his head pulling it tight. Dave placed his baseball bat horizontally across Johnny's ankles. Archie took a step back, "I'm going to love doing all your fucking joints, scum."

I could see Alfie lining up on Johnny's legs. He didn't move but for his efforts to catch breath in a tightened bag.

It was just then I heard the sound of a bugle, the US Cavalry Charge fanfare, as in all those cowboy films and series I'd seen as a child. Of course it wasn't anything like a bugle call. It was the sound of two rasping engines pulling through the archway. The first was a silver Pajero, a bit beaten up around the edges. Not as much as me, I suppose. It looked familiar. The other motor was some sort of Seat Estate. Or maybe Volkswagen, it was impossible to tell in those days.

Lenny whispered loudly in Johnny's ear. I could just hear above the shouts from the cars behind, "You've had a touch, lowlife. Lucky fucking Lucifer. If I ever see or hear you have been to London, I will finish the job and you will be dead! Got that?"

The all three of them disappeared around the corner of the garage to scale over some walls and find their walk back to any number of streets.

The next thing I remember clearly was Pedro sitting me in a chair in the open hall. I could hear Johnny talking to Pedro and calming him down. Some of the other three got some beers. "Was that the fucking surprise you meant in the car, Johnny?" I heard myself ask hoarsely.

Johnny looked at me. I thought it was something like relief. He smiled. "Bill fuck the beer, we'll go to whiskey. No the surprise was that it was our monthly yard party with lacheros – Pedro and the guys from the harbour. You hadn't forgotten had you Bill?"

I spent the rest of the evening getting patched up by some off-duty A&E nurse that Pedro knew. I was also helped by a few toots of the Peruvian marching powder. Johnny played cards and talked and laughed.

But I knew Lenny Reed would not forget about us. Now Johnny had to do something serious. Over the next day or two, I rested at Johnny's with thankfully no parties and no blond bimbos. While I was snacking on some tapas at the table overlooking the pool, Johnny wandered out with the phone clamped to his ear. "Look, Mr Elder you still get some good info on trucks coming in through the docks. Me and Bill are happy to stay out of London. But you gotta bring to the table what you promised. Just tell Mr Farringdon that I said, "Remember what I said about the Paddies and the Colombians". You both owe me and Bill."

That was the last it was mentioned.

Son of Lucifer

Chapter Eleven

The Visit

Lenny's office wasn't as busy as it had been before the Joe Wilkins scam. Lenny was behind his desk, looking at a file. Dave was looking over his shoulder, but they both looked up when they heard the brass knob turn in the panelled door.

For a second Lenny says nothing. Then a smile comes to lips, "Well, well. Mister Elder, or is it Detective Inspector now? What do I owe the pleasure? Fancy a flutter downstairs and seeking a tip?"

"Nah, I only bet on sure things. Just a polite visit, Len. I want to chat to you on your own. I think you'd prefer it that way," said DI Elder looking directly at Dave. Lenny nodded for Dave to leave.

As the door shut behind him, Mr Elder said brusquely, "Let's be clear from the get-go. I want Joe Wilkins left alone. I want Bill McFadden left alone. And if any of your mob shoot their mouth off about the matter, you'll be held personally responsible."

"What makes you think I have any interest in that grass?"

"I'm leaving Len. But let's put it this way. Anything happens to Joe Wilkins, then it happens to you. At the start it will be making life difficult for you. You know what Her Majesty's tax man can be like. But then it'll be me coming mob-handed."

Lenny said nothing, but he wasn't smiling. Elder continued, "And then, well and then Mr Farringdon will have to get involved. He wanted me to remind you of something, he said that you as choir boy should know the story. Something about Jesus telling a crowd to cast the first stone, publicity and that you still have responsibilities to him. How does that work, Len?"

Chapter Twelve
The Quiet Years

Mr Elder had bought us our lives. I, for one, was grateful and had no problems staying out of London. I also liked Johnny's idea of avoiding the drug dealing business for a while. He said there were plenty of other options and business to pick up on.

Over the next year or so, we went back into simple couriering from Morocco and transporting to the rest of Europe. We both had other things to do as well and now and again Johnny disappeared for days or even weeks at a time. My main job for him was to keep things ticking over – the club, boatyard and even his villa.

It was a damn sight less stressful for me than working with Johnny on drug deals. I paid the local Old Bill, kept the club running as a mainstay income. It was a little goldmine at the best of times. Let's be honest, with Johnny's contacts and reputation the drinking club attracted a lot of wealthy fun-loving cons. Costa del Crime lags and Moroccans and Colombians, tourists and wealthy Spanish. Me and Johnny knew how to run a club. And, as Johnny said to me years ago, what better a place to hear what is going on in the underworld, Than out of drunken mouths.

Then "any other business" was more about a "defensive investment position" as I later learned the ponce's in the investment banks called it. In other word's hang on to what we've got, except for filling any current deals and anything not already sold would be "stored". We were only doing small deals so that was always sorted quickly.

It was all business. No, Johnny was always smart about risk. He knew others would make bad decisions on what was risky or not. Not that he doesn't take his own risks and that he's not ruthless, he is, he was. No, Johnny was particularly good at assessing it. He could look at a situation from every angle, from every point of view. He'd look at the risks in the venture, how he could turn an apparently dire circumstance into a profitable deal, certainly in the longer run.

At least that's what I had assumed. Like I said Johnny disappeared on his own, then sometime around mid-August 1987, he seemed more furtive than usual. He'd taken a couple of boat trips, been to Morocco for a few days, a quick trip to Gibraltar. But he seemed to be in chipper form. We'd still have a quiet drink poolside at the villa and the lancheros monthly party had become something special.

Still I should have known. Up at the villa, in the club, out in the boat for bloody weeks he went around humming that blasted paddy tune, Danny Boy. There were times when I wished I'd had Alfie's four-pound club hammer.

Johnny had disappeared for about a week, when I got a call from London. It was Ian Ingrams, Johnny's old brief. "Ah hello Bill," purred Ingrams.

"Hello Mr Ingrams. And what do I owe for the pleasure of your call?"

There was a pause from the other end of the phone, as if to say, "what the fuck do you think I'm phoning about…" and I breathed, "Don't tell me its Johnny, Mr Ingrams. What's happened now?"

"Well Joe has got himself in a bit of bother, about one and a half million pounds-worth of bother and before you ask: no, Farringdon won't help on the charges. Customs made the bust off the coast of Sussex, so between them, the local plod and the coastguard cutters too many people know about it for it to just disappear," Ingrams summed up.

It was a tip-off to customs that Joe Wilkins was turning up with £1.5 million of top-quality Moroccan hash in a boat called the Danny Boy. Why he decided that he could overlook the Lenny Reed Health Advisory was beyond me. But knowing Joe he figured that Sussex wasn't London and he had someone else at the other end.

That still mystifies me. Who was he dealing with?

Anyway the way I look at it, I wouldn't have been surprised that Lenny found out something and grassed him up to customs. Bet Mr Elder and Mr Farringdon were pissed off with the whole thing. Johnny later said he'd got bored and had simply got the urge to go back to smuggling the old-fashioned way.

I bet money had something to do with it. It was obvious that this was not a job with Mr Elder at any point, otherwise customs would have been kept at bay.

Basically, I had a quiet life after Johnny got nicked. I kept in touch. And he always seemed optimistic in his monthly letter. I was to keep things running over as usual. While I got the run of Johnny's villa, I kept my own apartment. A year later I got another call from Ingrams. He said the court had landed Joe Wilkins with a ten year sentence.

Joe, Johnny, called me after a couple of months from HM Prison Ford, more commonly known as Ford Open Prison. He sounded remarkably upbeat for a man with a decade to serve. But I couldn't get my head round how he'd ended up in Category D prison. I mean it specialised in housing non-violent offenders with a low risk of absconding.

Anyway in 1991, Ingrams called again. "Bill, have you heard from Joe?"

"Ah no, should I have?"

"I've just been informed that he's walked out of Ford, he's done a fucking runner Bill."

I started laughing. "Good old Joe, bet he's been planning that for months. I wouldn't be surprised if he turns up in the bar in a couple of weeks. I'd better get the villa cleaned up."

"Makes my life a little more difficult. Anyway if he does turn up call me on the private line, Bill. Good luck," he finished.

It was a few months later that I got a call from Joe. He was calling from prison. "Howdy Bill, how's our business doing?"

"Fuck Joe, where are you calling from and how are you?"

"Ah Bill. Good to hear your voice. Yeah back inside, this time at Highpoint low security prison." He paused.

"I'm sorry you're back in, mate. You're fucking where? Highpoint? After doing a runner? You're one lucky fucker Joe," I spluttered.

"Yeah, you might say. I mean they've all got TVs in the room. There are classes – I've been brushing up on me Moroccan mate," laughed Joe. "Some change since the last time I was in during the 70s."

As incredulous as I must have sounded we continued talking for five minutes on business, a couple of suggestions for the club and some mates.

And that was it until January 1992. I was lying by the pool up at the villa. The phone rang and I picked it up from the glass side table. "Bill, it's Ingrams here. He's fucking done it again?"

"Done what Mr Ingrams?"

"He's done a fucking runner from Highpoint now."

"Really?" I said, trying not to laugh. I could tell he wasn't too happy about that reaction last time. "How did he do it this time?"

"They let him go to a dental appointment in London on his own. He never turned up. Do you think there might be a Lenny possibility?" asked Ingrams.

"Nah, Joe knows what he's doing. I'm sure he'll be in contact. Thanks for the call Mr Ingrams," I answered.

After I put the phone down, I picked up a fizzing champagne flute and turned to a paler, older friend, "Cheers Johnny, welcome home!"

Chapter Thirteen
A New Line of Business

The next couple of years were quiet. And boy did I love them. Plenty of women, sun, booze and enough drugs to keep me happy. We weren't really dealing any more but I did like coke for certain special occasions and I still had heaps left from what Johnny had already given me. Mind you Johnny was getting through what little we had left in Spain.

It didn't bother me. The fact Johnny was out, Lenny Reed seemed to be staying out of our way and not another word did we hear about Saeed, and I was a happy and contented man.

That's not to say we didn't get up to a bit of mischief. It was 1996. Apart from the Costa del Crime contingent bringing some right mugs in, there were all sorts of scams. I mean some of these big spenders never examined the bill. Nor were they drinking what they were paying for. It depended on the company and the time of the night.

I ran the nice little sideline of "recycling" shall we say. It was a small bottling plant. We could recork all sorts of bottles and put new screw caps on spirits. We used original bottles. That was easy enough to do. Big stupid spenders would get the royal treatment but after a few bottles of the good stuff they were getting the passable stuff. Maybe a bottle at a time or maybe a shot.

But I tell you what, we made a fucking bomb. I mean our genuine prices weren't cheap to begin with.

But then they didn't mind. Me and Johnny were good at clubs. I learned a lot from him.

And what Johnny had learned from running clubs also made him good at reading people, at getting people what they wanted, at picking up information and handling the criminal fraternity. His Uncle Bert ran an upmarket club in Berkeley Square called the Nightingale up until the 1960s. Bert had connections with the Anglo-Italian gang ran by the Sabinis, the boss Charlie Sabini was known as the king of the racecourse gangs.

Joe's first time inside was over how he got his club licences. How he ended up with the famous Winston's club remains open to question to this day. I know owner Bruce Brace always said he never got a penny for it, before Joe started running it. But I know no details.

His second stay at her Majesty's pleasure was, in 1976, for living off the immoral earnings of the prostitutes. In those day's he also ran a bunch of escort agencies out of Soho – Glamour International, Playboy Escort and La Femme. He was good at it.

Yeah Joe had taught Johnny all he needed to know.

I remember then exactly when me and Johnny did something which would have a critical influence on the direction of our lives.

It was in 1996. Johnny was standing at the bar. It was near central to the drinking area and far enough from

Son of Lucifer

the dance floor that you didn't get deafened. Johnny had put in state-of-the-art speakers and sound system. He wasn't quite the lady-killer in looks any more. That Michael Caine look had gone. That's to say he'd put on a few years around the chin and lost a few hairs from the top of his head. He also now sported a moustache. He hadn't put on pounds on the waist and still always looked casually dapper.

He was standing next to Saul Epstein. We all called him Saul but he said his friends in London all called him Solly. He was a retired diamond merchant who worked out of Hatton Garden and had lived in Golders Green. So you get the picture.

Saul was about 70 and one of those blokes that rarely talked about his problems. He listened well, said some sage things and joked a lot. He had a big belly laugh. Jovial, I guess that's how you'd describe Saul. He was about five foot six inches, obviously was well-fed by his wife, Maisie. We didn't see much of her, I don't think she was too well, but cheerful enough. One thing I remember about Saul is that he had fat fingers and it always used to mystify me how someone with such big fingers could handle and examine the delicate stones so easily.

Anyway they're looking at the activity in the club while leaning on the bar drinking beer. I remember it was too early in the day to hit whiskey or champagne and I was waving a newspaper at Johnny as I crossed the club floor avoiding seated punters. "Oi, Johnny, he's only here, mate."

Johnny looked irritated. "Who the hell you talking about?"

I grinned at him. "Ah that's why you need me Johnny-boy. Yeah it's only the geezer who won the UK lottery."

Johnny still had that mystified look. He obviously couldn't hear me above the music. He indicated for me to follow him into his office. The first thing he did after I closed the door was to reach into his desk pull out some coke and divide up two lines with his black Amex card. We both snorted.

"Now what were you on about?"

"Look this is the English language tourist paper saying this UK lottery winner is here in Costa del Sol," I said excitedly.

"So?"

"So I read about his win in the English papers. I remember it because he was the only winner on new year's Eve of the National Lottery – six point four million pounds. The paper here spotted the story and I spotted him," I gushed.

"Indeed, tell me more. I'd like to meet him but keep all this stuff from Saul," smiled Johnny.

"Sure, haven't mentioned it." After I'd ran into him earlier, I'd done a bit of research on Tom Papworth. He was 38, an ex-London ambulance driver who lived in Welwyn Garden City. And he'd had enough of London or was planning to leave he's wife and kids with the intent of living out here alone with his winnings.

After I'd briefed Johnny, I added. "The meet is already organised. He also mentioned that he's looking to buy on the Costa del Sol and was seeking advice. Just the same as Saul, I told him I know someone in the game: you!"

"Good man, Bill. Now let's try and keep Saul and Tom apart, as much as possible. Can you bring him in tomorrow night? Saul happens to be going back to London tomorrow."

Things always happen fast in Spain. Well they do if Johnny's paying for it. It was the next evening that Tom Papworth met Johnny Fay.

It might have been the evening, but Tom like a lot of Brits was still wearing sandals with socks. Not only that but his legs were whiter than his uninspiring shorts and highlighted by two red blotches on his knee-caps. He was even wearing a Union Jack tee-shirt for Christ sakes.

He had a full long face with a high forehead. He could have had a decent head of hair but it was greying and closely cropped. His chin was marked square with an almost chipped cleft in it.

I have to say, I liked Tom from the get-go. He was one of those "people persons". He had a taste of me and Johnny – knowing how to put people at their ease. But that's where any similarities ended. He was a trusting person.

"Well Tom this is Johnny Fay. He's the man in-the-know and can help you with property plans, introduce you to the right people. You want something, he will find it for you at the right price," as a way of introduction. "Johnny this is Tom."

The two shook hands firmly and Johnny had that smile. "Good to meet you. It's nice to have a man with good luck around, now how about a drink?" offered Johnny. He turned to Francesca, one of the many nubile girls we had serving, "Champagne all round. We have to celebrate Tom's good fortune."

I remember that immediately, Tom moved to the bar, "I'll get that Johnny."

"Oh no you won't old son. It's on the house. Your money's no good in here tonight, mate. My house rule this evening," he jokingly chastised. That was Johnny, he knew the score.

Tom became part of the furniture over the next few months. The first time he visited us, it was to suss the place out, but once Johnny had got him, there was no way he would move back to England. Sometimes he'd be back to England for a trip for a few months, but as the years went on, he spent most his time with us.

By buying that champagne for the millionaire, Johnny knew he'd won over Tom's heart. Tom had been hanging around the expat areas for a few weeks now and his fame went with him, which meant his cash. He told me once that the reason he liked Johnny, was that he was different. He wasn't a scrounger. He was generous to Tom.

I still have a cutting, I even showed it to Dr Graham.

It was an interview with Tom years later in the Evening Standard or the Daily Mail or some such rag and he told the journalist, "If I admired something, said I liked an item of clothing, John would buy it. He'd get out his black Amex card and buy it right on the spot. He was incredibly generous."

Tom was like an open book. To be honest he was his own worst enemy, it was like leaving the pub's keys with an alcoholic, you've only got yourself to blame for the results. By the time he was heading back to Blighty the first time, and due to come back in a couple of weeks, me and Johnny knew everything.

Yes he'd won £6.4 million. But he'd given away £2.4 to family and friends, including his divorced wife before he left for Spain. The rest was invested with Barclays Wealth Management arm. He figured in a place like Spain he could live comfortably for the rest of his life on £4 million.

What Johnny couldn't get his head around was that Tom had continued working in the ambulance service for a few months after his win. Tom just said he liked people and didn't want to let his team down.

I liked Tom. And I could see it was going to be a long-term project.

It was later that night, after the club had closed and Tom had been taken home in a taxi, that me and Johnny sat down in his office. We only did this occasionally. It was either left up to the staff, or me. If Johnny was partying at the villa, I usually followed on later.

"Well Bill, it's like London fucking buses."

"Eh?"

"It's like London buses – they all come at once – Saul, Tom and Kenny," said Johnny looking straight at me.

"Kenny?" I repeated with an obvious blank look on my face.

It was then he told me. Before meeting with Tom he'd had a phone call, "It was from Albert the Chop," he said.

"Wot? Albert who has the chop shop in Lewisham? I thought he was trying to keep his nose clean?" Albert the Chop was named well. Not only did he run a garage that specialised in pimping and redoing motors, he loved pork chops and his weapon of choice was a big machete. He said he'd developed an attachment to it after spending a year in Malaya during his National Service.

I knew Albert was trying to go straight but it often proved a problem for him. People liked his work both in the garage and as a get-away driver, so he was in demand. The other thing was that he was loyal and a lot of old hands trusted him.

"So what did he want, Johnny and please tell me Kenny isn't Ken Noye?"

"Bill I've always remarked how perceptive you are. It seems our Kenny has yet again been put upon by the forces of law and order. According to Albert he's killed a bloke after a row. Self -defence," explained Johnny.

"And that's got to do with us, what exactly?" I asked. I had met Kenny Noye a few times in Spain, always with Johnny. Let's put it like this, Kenny made me nervous, very nervous. If I thought Lenny Reed was dangerous, Kenny was in a league of his own. Lots of people disappeared around him and he had the means to pay for it. The thought of Johnny pulling a scam on Ken made me feel sick.

"Now Johnny, you're not thinking what I think you're thinking?"

"Now, now Bill, this is professional courtesy. He'll be turning up here at some point and when he does, I must show hospitality. Besides you know he's not short of a few bob and he'll be looking for somewhere to buy," said Johnny, clapping his hands together and rubbing them hard.

"I show courtesy Johnny, but if you're planning anything, just leave me out."

Oh Johnny was planning things.

But I was leaving him to it. Kenny was not to be trifled with. Let's put this in perspective. Now, I know a lot things about Kenny and about Brinks Mat and a few other stories, but I also know that people are still looking for some of the gold, including some of the new young guns. I also know Kenny is up for parole soon. Others of the gang have never been caught.

By the time I got around to telling Dr Graham the story, I knew that it had at least twenty bodies attached to it. Mine is not going to be another.

Are you sitting comfortably? Here's the shortened version. It was a cold Saturday morning in November in 1983. It was a typical warehouse on a typical trading estate near Heathrow and a blue Ford Transit was sitting outside. The six armed men knew this nondescript building had a vault and in the vault was a lot of money, up to three million pounds.

During the raid the staff of Brinks-Mat were cuffed and their shins wrapped tightly in heavy-duty duct tape. After they were hooded, they were threatened, pistol-whipped and beaten. Petrol was poured over one of the guard's groins. But as far as the gang were concerned, this was reasonable because it helped them hit the jackpot.

It wasn't £3 million. It was over £26 million in gold bars. The £400,000-worth of travellers cheques, diamonds and cash were a minor bonus.

This was the start of a very long saga. In the long run the haul financed several big and violent criminal gangs and has been blamed for unleashing ever more drugs into Britain, especially pushing ecstasy to its popular position amongst discerning drug users.

But the initial problem was how to get rid of the gold. This was where Kenneth Noye came in. Some say he was involved from the inception and financed the raid. I don't know anything about that, but he certainly was involved in smelting the gold and laundering it. He was good at it. Apparently he even managed to sell some of the re-smelted stuff back to the company who originally owned it – Johnson Matthey.

But the whole thing was beginning to get out of hand. In less than two weeks police arrested three of the raiders. It wasn't difficult to see why they collared some of them – they evidently weren't the brightest stars in the sky. One of them moved from a council house in Dulwich, to a mansion in Kent. He then got two Rottweiler's calling them Brink's and Mat. Duh!

But somehow they had also got onto Kenny. And that would become a headache.

Chapter Fourteen
Sorting Business

Johnny had a headache. He'd been out on the town with Tom, again. He liked his champagne, did Tom, but up until now all he'd had was £300 a week driving an ambulance in North London. For Tom it was time to move on from stress and people taking advantage. Johnny couldn't begrudge him the good life and neither could he disapprove, As he'd done it himself many a time. Also he needed to keep Tom onside. This was his second trip back and they were getting down to business.

Tom was either currently in one of Johnny's expensive bathrooms possibly with his head down the toilet, or still in bed. Johnny had business today concerning Tom and Saul, so either of those places would suit him. Keep him out of the way.

He was sitting in his villa's kitchen at the black marble-topped breakfast bar, drinking an espresso. He loved these new machines that made decent coffee. After all those years when starting the day meant starting the day with a good old cup of Rosie Lee and here he was fully converted to small strong coffees, like a Spaniard. Who'd have thought?

That's when his mobile phone rang. He looked at the number. It was a UK number. It looked familiar. Odd that he'd be getting a call at this time of day from London.

"Hello, Johnny Fay."

It was Detective Inspector Elder, "Johnny, hello, Johnny can you hear me? Long time no chat. You been keeping your head down? I'm sure Mr Farringdon would send his love if he knew I was phoning."

"Mr Elder, nice to hear from you. I can talk at the moment but may drop out at some point. Signal. What's happening?"

It suddenly dawned on him that he knew exactly what this was about. "Listen Johnny, Kenneth Noye. You know him?"

Johnny smiled to himself and straightened his back. "Kenny Noye the man with the golden gun, gold fingers, the man behind the mask…"

"Shut up, Johnny," Elder interrupted.

"Calm down Mr Elder. Yeah I know Ken, he's an old pal, why?" By this stage Johnny was shaking from unreleased laughter.

"I want him Johnny. Badly. He has stabbed a young man to death in Swanley, Kent… Road rage… but he is on his toes. If he turns up there I want to know about it. Got it?"

"Been a bit out of contact with home lately. I've not heard anything much about it here," Johnny lied.

"Okay Johnny don't forget you owe me son, big time, from sorting out Lenny Reed. All's been quiet on that front since, hasn't it?"

Johnny had stopped silently laughing and ran a hand

through his now-greying hair, thinking about Len's halitosis, his spit on Johnny's nose and the first whack from Alfie's hammer. Yeah he wasn't going to forget that too quickly.

"Yeah well that protection was nearly too late, wasn't it? Okay so what's in all this for me. It's dangerous, it's a mate and it'll cost," Johnny asked, his voice leaden serious, now.

"One of the red tops has put up a £50,000 reward for the capture of Noye. Plus the Lad's family have stuck up £20,000. I don't want any of it and can send it your way... I just want him," Elder half-shouted, half-pleaded.

"You lot really can't forgive him for killing one of your own, eh?"

"It's got nothing to do with that," snapped Elder. "It's a bad thing he's done to a hard working Lad and his family. The man's an animal, this wasn't business and it wasn't amongst gangsters. It was out of order."

"Okay, okay. The man's a pal but business is business. If I hear anything, I'll contact you but it might be some time, you know how it goes, besides I'd also be checking Cyprus if I were you," Johnny told Elder. "Adios Mr Elder," he hung up.

He sat back and thought about it. Grassing up Ken could be a risky business. He didn't know any details about this latest escapade, but it must have been bad to get Elder so upset. No one in the business could forget Kenny's unbelievable bit of luck when he managed to kill an undercover copper by stabbing him ten times but got off. The unlucky Detective Constable John Fordham was dressed in camouflage watching Noye at home. When Noye's dogs started barking at something in his garden, Kenny-baby went out with a kitchen knife, found Fordham and in self-defence did him.

Also what the fuck was Kenny doing to get himself banged up again? He'd only just got out. Six months after he got off the murder charge, he got charged with VAT fraud over the Brink's Mat gold and got 14 years. The Old Bill found gold bars at Kenny's place when they were investigating the Fordham thing. The government and the insurer's lawyers also managed to fleece him of nearly £4 million when he was inside. He only got out a couple of years ago, but I suppose after losing all that money, you'd be mad too.

He was woken from his reverie as Tom's flip-flops clattered across the tiled floor. "Christ! My thumping head. What time is it Jon?" Tom croaked.

"Twelve o'clock. Midday. Listen. I have to go out for a while, Tom, to see some people on your behalf, sort a few things out. You know," Johnny told him.

Tom scratched his head and yawned, "Do you need me with you?"

Johnny smiled at Tom and his general level of dishevelment. "Ha, by the looks of you, you're in no fit state to go anywhere at the minute, are you mate? No just some initial groundwork."

Tom tried to nod in agreement, but one slight move

forward brought on swimming eyes and unbearable pressure to the brain. Even his smile was forced.

"I'll leave you to go and recover," said Johnny.

Half an hour later Johnny and his Bentley Coupe drew up outside Antiguo Bar Nuevo in Plaza Casares. He always liked Casares and it was away from prying eyes. His business was private. The village was less than twenty miles from Estepona but it hugged the cliffs of the high mountain pass. In the distance one way was the azure blue of the sea, the other the magnificent ruggedness of the mountains.

The whole village was like stepping back in time. The town had grown around a 12th century castle, and on the highest hill sat a church. From a distance it looked like a geometric puzzle, uniformly white boxes of varying height and width all trying to face southwards seemingly perched perilously on mountain sides. It may not have had much architectural imagination each roof red-tiled, every wall perfectly white, but the homogenised walls were interrupted with protruding balconies, others with delicately arched covered terraces, full length windows or shuttered wooden ones. The Moorish influence was everywhere.

He could see the others waiting for him on the roof terrace as instructed. He loved this bar too. It was like a bank building in white. For two feet from the bottom was brown marble faced blocks, then the traditional white render. Stonework arched over the rich brown wooden door. All the downstairs windows had wooden shutters; the second floor had closed off windows, leaving one balcony inaccessible, while the third floor had two full length windows with wrought iron Juliet balconies.

He liked the roof terrace as could look down into the small square and watch all the comings and goings in front of him. Actually it was more of a triangle really.

There were only the four of them on the terrace when they started. This was Johnny's team for the sort of work he'd pulled time and again in recent years. It was his Winning Team, yep the Winners.

Juan, Oliver and Mark were his Winners. He realised it had been a bit of a bonus when he'd run into Mark Lufton. He was a man of few morals, a true estate agent, a true Liverpudlian, thought Johnny.

The four of them sat on padded wooden chairs around a circular table with a bright white crisp table cloth. They had the table closest the wrought iron and stone balustrade, sheltered from the direct sunlight by a vine-covered trellis.

Johnny had spent half an hour outlining his plan. There were few questions from the other men because they knew the drill. He took another sip of his red wine and then said, "That's about it for the minute. Mark, I will need you straight away though. You need to find an apartment. Three-bed, nice area, somewhere near my place would be good."

Mark nodded and Johnny noticed flecks of grey hair appearing on his temples for the first time. "There's a project going up two blocks from yours, I will talk to the developer. He is a good pal of mine, I'm sure we can stitch something up," said Mark, brightly.

Then Johnny turned to lawyer Juan. He was the only man that came to Johnny's parties out of the Winners and he knew who Johnny dealt with. He kept that knowledge away from these workmates, better they didn't know just how dangerous Johnny could be.

"Are we going to be all right on the legal front, Juan? There can't be any slip ups, otherwise it's all but a pointless exercise," asked Johnny, leaning forward.

Juan sounded as collected as he looked, immaculate jet black hair, manicured nails and his perfect English. "Have I ever let you down Johnny?"

"No. And you better not on this one. It's too important. Got it?"

"Okay, Johnny. I got it, the paperwork will be perfect."

Oliver sat forward at this point. He looked what he was. Going bald, a rounded face with a ruddy complexion from too much wine, too much sun and too much work, Oliver worked in the local wealth management division of a large British bank, Bartons. His earnest approach and public school accent had helped him bring in clients. But so had Johnny.

"So I suppose I come in on the transaction side, old boy?" he piped.

"Yeah, all transactions. Ollie you just stay where

I can contact you, when I need you… old boy," Johnny mimicked.

All three of them began to laugh. Johnny had got it off to a tee. It was as Mark leaned across the table to take the chilled wine from its bucket and pour himself another drink, that Johnny noticed Toni.

Sitting at a table by herself at the back of the terrace. Johnny could not believe he had not seen her coming up the stairs and sitting down. She was stunning. Her long, silky, straight black hair hung down her back, her sunglasses perched on top. Her olive skin was tanned and radiated health. She had what seemed like huge brown eyes and the prefect face, her features symmetrical and unblemished.

Johnny estimated that she was in her late twenties early thirties, maybe Italian. She looked Italian and she dressed with Italian flair, a simple dress cut to every curve of her body with a low back and modest front, unable to hide the large breasts struggling to be free.

Johnny was surprised by his reaction to her. Most of the girls he lusted after were blond. Bill had told him they all looked like his ex-wife, Pearl. Pearl. He had noticed her when her career as a swimwear model began to take off in the 60s. It wasn't just her 36-24-36 figure, she was also good-looking and she was tough. By the time they were married he had her running one of his London escort agencies and when he was jailed for three years on vice charges, Pearl was later convicted of assisting in the running of an escort agency.

She spent no time inside but she'd had enough of Joe. He remembered how he'd felt when he first heard that she was seeing Queen's Park Rangers soccer boss David Bulstrode. That memory snapped him out of thinking about Pearl. He got up from his chair, excusing himself from those at the table.

Johnny could feel a hint of excitement, the hunt was on. As he neared her table, a waiter came up the stairs and left a silver saucer with her bill on it. Still not noticing Johnny, Toni picked up the bill to look at it, when his hand touched hers gently, grasped the bill and a voice said, "No one as beautiful as you, should be spending your own money. Please allow me to pay".

Toni looked up at Johnny and smiled. She squinted slightly at the sun's glare, wrinkling her nose and without hesitation said, "If you insist." She paused, "Sorry I never got your name or is it the White Knight?"

Johnny smiled, reached into his hip pockets and unfurled a corpulent wad of peseta notes, pulled a few off and left them on the saucer. He still said nothing as he pulled an embossed business card from his shirt's top pocket and placed it deliberately in front of Toni.

As he turned to walk away he paused casually and said, "My name is Johnny Fay, darling.

And that is where you will find me."

Chapter Fifteen
Hello Kenny

It had been an exhausting couple of weeks, at least as far as Johnny was concerned. He couldn't believe he had just stayed at home for the past two days. He did nothing but relax. He hadn't heard from Mr Elder. He hadn't heard from Albert and he hadn't heard from Kenny.

He wasn't surprised. Even if Kenny was coming to see him, it could take him some time to make it down here. It depended on all sorts of things. He might have to go elsewhere to pick up some running money. He might not have left England quite as sharpish as Mr Elder and Albert thought he was going to.

Things hadn't been finished with Tom yet either and it was now 1997. He was coming back in a week or so and Mark had lined him with a nice little apartment that should see a bit of cash flow coming into Johnny's coffers.

He was sitting in his arched room at the table reading the Daily Telegraph. He liked reading the court pages and reports. It kind of kept him up to date with what was going on at home. Then, through the arches he heard the swish of car tyres sweeping in the gate and around the gravel drive. He got up and went to the bar a pushed a button on a TV monitor. Since the Lenny experience he had installed a few cameras around to beef up security. As the screen flickered on, he heard the thump of a car door closing.

He recognised the short cut blond hair, the five foot eight frame and the walk. Johnny went through his dining room towards the front door. The heavy iron knocker clattered a determined demand for access.

Johnny swung one of the doors open, gave a big smile and greeted his visitor effusively. "Kenny baby what's been happening? I was expecting you months ago. Not a call, not a postcard, don't ya love me any more?"

Kenneth Noye dropped his bag, laughed and hugged Johnny. "Good to fucking see you, Johnny and I already like the pad."

Johnny picked up Kenny's bag put it inside the hallway and put an arm around his shoulders. "Leave that mate, we're going to sit outside and have a nice relaxing beer." He directed Kenny through the house pointing out where things were on the trip to the arched room, and then settled down by the pool.

"Cheers," said Kenny as he clinked his bottle of San Miguel with Johnny's. "Thanks for this mate. As soon as I sort some monies out Joe, I will look after you. It's been a hectic few months but I'm getting my ducks lined up."

"No problems. Treat the villa as your own, mate. Me casa su casa, as they say around here. Relax. Do a bit of swimming, soak up some rays, have a few drinks, watch telly and sleep. You look like you could do with it. Particularly bad day then?" Johnny asked sympathetically.

"Bad fucking year, mate. I was running about the last few weeks pulling some monies out of things and I have to pick something up later," replied Kenny sourly.

"Well look, it's just as well you caught me here. I have to go out now and meet Bill. You remember Bill MacFadden?" Kenny grunted assent.

"I'll be at the club later. Phone me, yeah? It's on the business card you have," continued Johnny.

"All right Joe. I will call you later. I think I'll just jump in the shower first, make a few calls and maybe have a nap," said Kenny.

"See you later, then," said Johnny.

As Johnny pulled away from the villa in his Bentley, he considered calling Mr Elder. Maybe he should update him. Nah, fuck it. Let it ride for a while, Kenny could be a good little earner for a few months.

It was quite some time later that Johnny saw Kenny again and it gave him a start. It was after midnight at the club and while it had thinned out in terms of numbers, some of the more dedicated punters were clinging tightly to whatever element of sobriety they retained. Johnny always noticed the burble of chat and laughter got louder and louder as the evening went on. He was letting Bill entertain the regulars tonight, as he still felt drained from the last few weeks' activity and was keeping his distance sitting in a corner table that gave a view of most of the club. He had some ledgers in front of him, using them as a polite 'do not disturb' notice.

Then he saw Kenny Noye enter. He stood by the

front door surveying the room, assessing the clientèle and the club's layout. Before he had moved from where he'd come in, Johnny was by his side, using his body to shield him from others looking over.

"Kenny, Kenny, Kenny. Thought you were going to give me a phone call? C'mon let's go to the office, bit of privacy there," he said.

As they walked to the back, Johnny taking the less populated and darkest route, he saw Bill looking up from the bar and clocking Kenny. Bill turned away and resumed chatting to the three people in front of him.

Inside the office Johnny felt more relaxed. "You feeling a bit better, Ken?"

"Yeah, it's a great pad. But the reality is I got to find somewhere of my own, Joe. Bit fed up of crashing here and there and fancy some time to myself. I'm even considering buying," confided Kenny.

"Oh really. Well we'll talk about that later. But there are a few things we've got to get straight. Out here everyone knows me as Johnny Fay. You know what I mean? It's important. As for a place, that's no problem. I've already sorted something, got you a small villa all to yourself mate. It's two thousand pound a month, three months up front. It has its own pool and will be empty until Winter. I know the people who own it," said Johnny, gleefully.

He threw down two sets of keys on his desk, one with a tag on it with the villa's address, the other with a Wrangler tagged logo.

Son of Lucifer

"Now, look one is for the villa, the other is for a Wrangler Jeep. It comes with the villa, so no problems with it looking out of place being parked on the drive. On top of that it's only two minutes away from mine. How's that for you?"

Kenny released a deep breath. "Fuck that was quick. You're a real pal, Joe... I mean

Jon. I owe you, mate," he said gratefully, reaching forward and pocketing the keys.

"Okay another thing, Kenny. My home is open to you anytime and we'll socialise there. There are too many faces get in here, you know, some of the old hands. There are also a lot of tourists and with your mug being all over the papers I'd say it's best to keep clear of the club," he counselled. "You get what I mean. But the villa is always open to you. As I said, treat it as your own. We can talk there too."

"Yeah, you're right. Some of those old lags would sell their grandmother. You can't trust anyone, any more. In that case, is there a back way out? I'll see you back at your place," Kenny said resignedly.

"Naturally, and you'll find the Jeep out there too," said Johnny as he took a bunch of keys from the draw of the desk and unlocked a barely noticeable door in the back corner of the room. An unusually cool gust of the nights breeze wafted in and while Kenny made his way to the Jeep, Johnny stood watching, looked up to the stars and took a deep breath.

Son of Lucifer

Chapter Sixteen

Whatever You Say, Kenny

I'd spotted Johnny creeping through the club with Kenny. The fact that he'd obviously left by the back exit, meant Johnny wanted to keep him out of sight, which was all right by me. I'd met Kenny a couple of times when he was taking a holiday this end of the country. He made me nervous.

I'd already made it clear to Johnny that I was not participating in any plans he might have for him. I'd also done a little poking around to find out what he'd done.

It was pretty vicious even for him, although some would say par for the course. In May 1996 somewhere close to his home in Swanley in Kent on an M25 slipway, a small red Bedford Rascal van swerved in front of his Land Rover Discovery. I dunno what had gone on that morning or whether it was simply that he hadn't eaten lunch or it was Kenny being Kenny, but he wasn't having it.

I suppose it wouldn't come as a complete surprise that it was a blond woman driving. Evidently pretty badly for Kenny. He followed the van blasting his horn and flashing his lights. Somewhere nearer Swanley after following them a mile or two, Kenny's patience ran out completely. He overtook the van, pulled in front and blocked it from going any further.

As he got out swearing at the female driver, her fiancée got out from the passenger side. I heard the two were infatuated with each other and were only going for a late lunch of bagels. It's only natural a man will look after his 19-year-old missus and this lad, an electrician, obviously thought he had the measure of Kenneth Noye. He was 21, over six foot and some four inches taller than a gobby 50-year-old. He probably thought, "If this bloke wants some, I'll have him."

The two of them stood in the road shouting at each other, no doubt a few "fucks" and "cunts" and "bastards" swapped in a dick-swinging competition. But whether Kenny had a flashback to that copper John Fordham, or there was one too many "cunts", he hit the lad, Stephen Cameron. As the lad staggered and his missus, Danielle, climbed out of the van weeping and screaming at them, no one saw where it came from. As usual Kenny was straight to the point and gave him a four inch blade, right into the heart and liver.

I heard she was cradling the lad as he bled, screaming. Cars kept driving around them and Kenny smiled at her, just turned around, got his Land Rover and fucked off. The kid never regained consciousness.

So it seemed to me that my policy of generally avoiding him because I had assumed he was a man of little patience was spot on. I'd managed it for a couple of days.

But today wasn't going to be one of those days. I had picked Johnny up from some office or other and

Son of Lucifer

we were returning to Johnny's villa to take Tom flat hunting. I was along for moral support for Tom and his search for a new life in Spain. Johnny just wanted me along to make sure his cash registers went 'ka-ching'.

When we walked through his villa out to poolside, Kenny was mixing himself a drink. He nodded to me when he saw me, but immediately hissed at Johnny. "I've been waiting for you Joe. But who's the idiot?"

Johnny threw a look to the door from the villa, winced and put his finger to his lips. Before he could say anything else Kenny continued, "He was here when I came over this morning and opened the door like he owned the gaffe. Who the fuck is he?"

"Don't worry, he's a little protective of me but he's just a mark. Please don't make him uncomfortable Ken or you'll cost me a few bob. What name did you give him?" asked Johnny.

"Don't worry, I used Peter Smith," answered Kenny.

I could see Johnny taking a deep breath. He wanted to use words like 'idiot', 'wanker' but thought better of it and in an exasperated tone snapped, "No. My name!"

"Oh, I only asked if Johnny was here."

"Good, that's cool. You remember Bill?"

I nodded again to Kenny and he looked at me for longer this time, "Okay Bill. Long time. Look Joe I've got something for you to be going on with."

Johnny looked at a bag sticking out from behind the bar and nodded to me to watch the door and for Tom who was somewhere in the house. I watched Kenny pull out bundles of money and set them on the top of the bar. The cash bundles were in thousands and Kenny started counting them out and put them into piles; six thousand, five thousand another twenty thousand. Fuck, what had Johnny been up to with him?

"All right, here's the six thousand for the villa, another five thousand for the motor and twenty grand for you helping out, is that okay?" asked Kenny.

I could see Johnny's eyes light up – cash, sweet-smelling new cash. Mmmmm. Almost jerking himself back into the moment physically, he humbly asked Kenny, "You sure?" But he was already picking it up and heading for the villa door and his bedroom and the safe.

Before he left the room, he turned and asked Kenny, "Are you are staying around, I mean you are going to make use of the villa you've just paid for?"

"Well, I really can't see me going back home. It seems I've upset a few people and it looks like I am here to stay, mate. So you will be seeing a lot of me about."

"Good, I mean it'll be good to have you here mate, And remember, anything I can do…" said Johnny.

Kenny picked up his bag and headed out to the pool to go through the garden to the drive but paused, "I know mate. It was good of you to let me use your contacts and don't worry, I will be in touch. I'm hoping you might be able to help me buy a pad down in Atlanterra. We can go eat one night next week yeah?"

Johnny nodded and left for his bedroom. Kenny nodded to me and walked under the arches to his parked Jeep.

It was only minutes before Johnny returned. "Tom's finishing in the shower, I could hear him, he'll be down in a minute," he told me.

Moments later Tom appeared in the doorway, short hair damp, chin showing bright signs of a close shave and redness from a too hot shower. "Hey. Your mate gone? He's a really nice bloke. We had a good chat."

Johnny looked at me and rolled his eyes. I couldn't help but smile.

"Yeah that's er Peter, a really nice bloke. Anyway how was it last night mate, enjoy yourself did you?" agreed Johnny, smiling at me again.

It was only then I could hear the clatter of heels coming down the stairs. Ah, that was Tracy. Myself and Johnny had only been around for the early stages of Tom's night out, organised by us of course. He'd latched on to Tracy early in the night.

She was a good-looking 45-year-old with long auburn hair and very good skin for a woman of her age. She also looked pretty fit. "Hello Bill," then she nodded to Johnny, gave a big smile while fiddling with her hair.

"I've never – I mean never – had a night out like that in my entire life. I'm sure it won't be the last," said Tom.

"Remember, you're in Spain now son. This how we do it over here. Anyway we've to go look at that apartment on the new build. You might as well stay here with me 'till it's completed" offered Johnny.

"How long is the completion date on the build?"

"About three months… That's if you like it, of course," Johnny replied, a little too obsequiously to my ears. But it worked, and nauseatingly Tom's reply was equally fawning, "I'm sure if it's anything to do with you, it'll be great. Can't wait to see it. You're a real mate Jon."

And that was it. Effectively. We traipsed off to the site, looked at some models and computer generated pictures and then had a good butcher's around a similar sized show apartment as Tom was interested in. It was all the usual guff you'd expect from an agent – Mark, the scouse bloke Johnny had become attached to. He even had the clipboard.

I could hear Tom playing the sensible punter and asking Mark what he thought were searching questions. Johnny threw in a few technical bullshit questions too – always to help Tom.

"So how much does it cost finished with the all-in price, Mark?"

"Ah the important question. Okay, with the best finish interior, it comes out at just under 70 million pesetas. That's just over three hundred and five thousand pounds. But you must understand that to anyone else the price is over ninety million pesetas," said Mark, speaking in a low voice. "But you do realise you can't say anything to anybody about prices, as Johnny here

Son of Lucifer

has introduced you to me, and as such I have done this favour for Jon… You understand, Mr Papworth?"

"I understand. I'll take it Mark. Get the paperwork ready for me to sign, and like I said, don't worry, mum's the word." Tom was grinning like the proverbial Cheshire cat.

"I'll get it over to your lawyer. Who is representing you, Mr Papworth?" Mark asked innocently, pen at the ready.

Johnny stepped forward, "It'll be Juan Rodriguez looking after Tom's interests, Mark. I'll give you his contacts."

"No problems," replied Mark, doing his best to avoid looking at Tom and Tracy now cuddling and pecking at each other like two white doves. After a second or two Tom catches himself, looked at Johnny and Mark beaming, "Right off for a celebratory drink, then?"

I congratulated him, linked my arm in his and Tracy's and walked them towards the exit, offering them a choice of exciting hostelry for us to retire to. As I moved them away I could feel Johnny move to Mark's side behind me.

That's when I knew Johnny and Mark were going over the final details and not just for the apartment sale. "Make sure the paper work is dual-ownership, but his name only on his copy, same as last time, got it?" insisted Johnny.

And that was that.

Son of Lucifer

Chapter Seventeen
M'Boy, M'Boy

Sometimes foreigners who live in Spain forget what day they have. Sunny, again. Hot, again. Same bar, again. Same drink, same people to chat to and it even sounded like the same music.

That is what it had seemed to Johnny for the past few weeks. Tom was still staying with him, which could get exhausting. It was like watching a kid discovering how to walk, discovering how to bang a drum and discovering how to wind up Dad – they just kept doing it because of the novelty and because they could. Tom was like that with the partying and since he'd met Tracy he was also on a mission to impress. At least his skin was no longer whitewashed.

Johnny was concentrating on the new cash injection into his bank account. In fact it was to be several new cash injections.

He had been in contact with Kenny since and was making discrete inquiries about property in Atlanterra. It was about two hours away in Cadiz province and while it wasn't everyone's cup of tea, Kenny liked the idea that it was a private residential development with luxury hotels, chalets, restaurants and sandy beach. It suited Kenny's state of mind. It was private and access was by a single road leading south from a small fishing village, so no through traffic and bordered by military land and salt marshes. Fortress Kenny, he had thought.

But what Kenny would cough up was just a small tip compared to what Johnny was eventually expecting from Saul and Tom.

It was only when Bill nudged him that he remembered he was still on-duty and was with Tom. The club was busy tonight with a special DJ he'd brought in from England. It was wall-to-wall women all doing their best to look like something out of Vogue, some succeeding better than others. Most of the men looked like they had money. Of course you always got the tourists who managed to get in, but generally evenings meant no shorts or sleeveless tee shirts.

Fortunately since Tom had met Tracy, he hadn't required as much hand-holding, so to speak, from Johnny and was sitting at a VIP table with his girlfriend.

It was then Johnny saw Toni. The long black silky hair sweeping from side-to-side as she looked around the club, peering into the darkness. She looked exquisite, drifting between the crowds, looking and finally seeing him. She waved and smiled broadly.

Bill noticed Johnny stand straighter with a big smile on his face and followed his eyeline to a goddess in a white dress weaving through the punters. He could see an angelic face, big eyes looking at Johnny. She wasn't pouting or looking coyly at him but with an intense interest.

As she drew up to Johnny's side this apparition of beauty waved in her hand a white card at Johnny. "Ah we meet again beautiful," he said. "I'd introduce you to my friend Bill here, but I still don't know your name."

Bill looked on wondering where Johnny had met this vision. He couldn't take his eyes off her and for once was lost for words but Johnny briskly warned him, "Staring Bill."

She laughed. "My name is Antonia... but you can call me Toni." She spoke softly, a hint of an accent. While Bill gulped out his own greeting, Johnny asked, "Drink? What would you like?"

"White wine... a decent chilled glass, please, Johnny."

Johnny lifted his hand up and signalled the barman. Roberto was a cousin of Pedro's but had been trained in clubs in London and while the bar was busy, he knew that keeping Bill and Johnny happy was his prime role. Other staff could run around after the others. He knew that Johnny wanted the expensive white, one of the estate bottles Vino de Pago registered.

Johnny picked up his drink, smiled at her and said, "Follow me Toni."

The two wound their way around the bar towards the back of the club to the office. Bill watched closely as they went under the sweeping black drapes, past the trellis wall that lead there and to some other private rooms. As Johnny unlocked the door he looked back to the bar and saw Bill's intent look.

Johnny nodded to the sofa set along one wall.

"Please, sit down. That drink will be here in a minute." Toni had only just sat down, when there was a gentle tap at the door.

"Ah, here it is," he said triumphantly as he turned and opened the door. Roberto was standing patiently outside with a napkin hung from his right arm and also balancing a tray. "Gracias, Roberto," Johnny nodded, as he took the tray that had another scotch for himself and a large glass of chilled white wine and the bottle in a silver wine bucket.

He passed the glass to Toni. "Thank you my white knight," she said, taking a sip. "Mmm, full-bodied, toasty oak and fruity – a Verdejo white grape, I'd say, from the Rueda region, north of Madrid. Not quite as good as an Italian pinot grigio"

"I see you know your wine," said Johnny. "But you do play hard to get don't you?"

"If you mean, am I easy? No I am not. I'm surprised at you," she replied with a slight tone of defiance.

"Sorry, what I meant was how long you've left it to come and find me. I wasn't being rude to you. It's just that it's been quite a while since I saw you at that restaurant in Casares," he said quickly, determined to head off any upset.

"Ah well, family business comes first with me. So I've been busy and now I've some time to see a bit more of Spain, so here I am," she replied smiling.

Johnny moved to sit beside her, feeling a shiver of excitement as if he was a young boy of sixteen again, but at that moment his desk phone rang. Toni noticed a flash of irritation on his face, as he turned to answer it.

"Sorry Johnny, but this is important. Saul has come in and is looking for you. I think he needs a bit of hand-holding on the Villa deal, mate. What do you want me to do?" whispered Bill from the bar phone.

"Oh bollocks. I suppose business is business. Send him through to the office and keep him away from Tom," said Johnny.

He couldn't believe that after waiting so long for this angel to turn up, he was going to ask her to leave in order to reassure a 70-year-old Jew. "Listen I'm really sorry Toni. I have to meet someone who's turned up about some business I'm doing. Unscheduled, of course. Can you do lunch tomorrow? When I'm here, it's working all the time or at least be on-call."

Toni smiled and dropped her eyes to show she was disappointed at this. "Oh okay. No, no, I understand. Look it's no bother. Lunch sounds good. But don't let this happen too often, will you Johnny?"

As she got up to leave, she scribbled her mobile phone number on the desk pad, picked it up and placed it directly into Johnny's hand. He held onto her hand and clasped it with his other. "What I mean is, you deserve my full attention Toni and you shall have it."

He gently kissed the back of her hand and then looked directly into her eyes. As Toni left the office, Saul paused to let her past and then, like so many men, watched her as she walked towards the bar.

He glanced at Johnny with an apologetic look, "Sorry Jon. It looks as if I've interrupted something?"

"No Saul, don't worry. Come in. Come in and sit down. What can I do for you?"

"Well I'm all ready for the big move. I spoke to Mark today and he said I can move into the place in two weeks – That's if Juan does the paperwork in time," Saul explained.

"There'll be no problems there. I'll speak to Juan first thing tomorrow. And your other half Saul? How's she taking the move?" asked Johnny gently.

He raised his hands, palms to heaven, "Ahh, you know women, Jon. All she's worried about is the pension, you know? will it be enough to live on out here."

"Now, now don't worry Saul. I'm always here to help. If anything like a bit of business turns Up I'll put you into it with me. Okay?"

"Oi, oi, you've been most generous to me, helping me buy the villa cheap, letting me use your contacts. You've been like a son to me," said Saul.

"Nah, that's what friends are for Saul. I'm sure you'd do the same for me. Go on get back to the little woman and leave it to me," said Johnny as he got up and walked over to the office door. Saul stood next to him and pushed his hand out, Johnny grasped it and gave it a solid shake. Saul brushed past him back into the darkness of the club while Johnny paused in the doorway staring at the bar area. Bill was sitting next to Toni and they were talking animatedly, Toni throwing her hair back and laughing.

It was less than two weeks later that Johnny saw Saul again, this time at his new home. Saul's villa was like so many others – whitewashed, red tiled roof, two storeys, surrounded by a five-foot high wall, garden planted to withstand the damning daily heat and lack of rainfall. It certainly wasn't as mature as Benny's garden but then it's new, thought Johnny when he arrived.

He went through the front door into a large hallway, ignoring the mezzanine floor above or the doors to the side. Within minutes Johnny was lying by the pool, his weathered skin taking another dose of Andalucian sunshine. Through his aviator sunglasses the blue sky looked orange but clear, not even a wisp of cloud. Beads of sweat sat along his forehead unmoving because he was horizontal on a green sunbed and next to him sat Saul.

Saul sat sideways on, feet on white tiles, flip-flops pointing penguin-like. He was looking at Johnny intently through his own sunglasses. His open multi-coloured shirt hinted a flabby belly and the greying chest hairs of an hirsute man. Johnny had been listening to Saul reminisce, drifting in and out of his own daydream of Toni and grunting at what seemed appropriate points.

Saul sighed deeply. "You know, when I was dealing Johnny, I had the respect of many in the business. And credit, oy vay the credit, I could have up to a million pounds of credit at any one time. In my business trust was the best way to assess risk. Oh yes, a million pounds of credit."

Naturally anyone pays attention when someone mentions a million quid, but Johnny had an in-built cash radar and even had he been in deep sleep, this comment would have swam through his unconsciousness and slapped its oily tail in his greedy face. Johnny actually stirred himself, struggled up on one elbow and then swung himself around to face Saul.

Just then through double patio doors and from the shade of a hanging awning came Maisie. He always thought she looked thin, even for her small stature. He could imagine her making great chicken soup, as she clucked around Saul and his guests at every opportunity. She was the best of conservative, a long floral dress, tied at the waist, her hair done up in a bun, practical for the temperature.

She made her way to Saul and Johnny with some concentration as she balanced a jug of cloudy lemonade, two glasses and a bowl of ice on a tray. He could hear her unsteady hands as the ice rattled gently. The speed at which she laid it on the small table next to the two men, sounded as if the exertion had reached its limit.

She paused for a second after she straightened herself and as breezily as she could said, "Here you are, boys… Enjoy."

Johnny smiled and thanked the old lady, but immediately his attention went back to Saul. Now was the time to lay some groundwork for possible future projects.

"Well just because you've come down here, there's no reason why you don't deal a little bit now and again. It'd pay your living costs wouldn't it, then you're not spending your own pension, eh, Saul?" advised Johnny. He sipped his lemonade and winced inside. Where's the fucking vodka he thought?

Saul was speaking. "The out-goings would cripple me, setting up a new business, registering the VAT. Besides I am an old man. Who wants the stress any more? I mean look at where we are… a cool lemonade, an inviting clear pool and the sun shining."

"Fair dues, but still have a think about it. There might be a move out there Saul, where we could earn you some money. I'd probably come in with you, but in the meantime if you ever need any money, give me a shout," said Johnny, leaning over and patting Saul's big hand.

Saul looked down at Johnny's hand and laid his other on top. "Ah my boy, you've been very good to us. I really like you but you have done enough for us. I could never repay you for the help you've given me," said Saul.

Johnny withdrew his hand and lay back down on the lounger, "Well remember if you need me for anything I'm here." He went back to daydreaming, not of Toni but of sparkling diamonds.

Son of Lucifer

Chapter Eighteen
Ka-Ching Again

Like I said before, you can get lost in the days in Spain. I took time now and again to pop up to Gibraltar for a change of scene and do some business. I started getting into fishing, I guess as you get older even to someone like me, the simple things in life become more attractive. Besides it wasn't as if I didn't have access to a boat. But life was mostly the same old, same old.

One thing that had changed was Toni.

I could tell that she was something special to Johnny. He was taking his time with her when she was here, wining and dining her and being unusually patient about, to put it bluntly, getting her into bed. I could understand his infatuation. Toni was a breath of fresh air around the club. She was intelligent but didn't make an issue of it. She was perceptive and seemed to get the measure of the club regulars. She had a great sense of humour and took an interest in people.

On top of that she was a stunner.

Yeah, I could tell Johnny liked her. Like I said Johnny's types had always been blondes with big tits. That's not to say Toni wasn't well endowed. But there was always, what I called the Pearl-type – they always reminded me of Johnny's ex-wife. Let's put it into perspective when Toni was around it was about the same year that Pearl managed to become the 1998 poster girl for Age Concern. "'Wonderbra' granny Pearl, the stunning 56-year-old with the 36-24-36 figure," according to the Daily Mirror. Johnny stopped reading the Mirror after that.

Oh course the one problem Johnny faced was that Toni was in and out of Spain regularly and he was busy. When he was dealing with his usual series of bimbos, they'd come and go, lie by the pool all day, whatever and didn't need tending by Johnny. Business came first with Johnny and currently that meant keeping an eye on Tom. It was only weeks until the apartment came through, but he had already been formulating another plan, or shall we say set of plans, to relieve Tom of some of his cash.

Even so I was always there to chat to Toni when he was busy. I liked her company. I mean it wasn't hard for it to be better than listening to a bunch of old boys reminisce about the jobs they pulled, the teeth they pulled and which weapon they favoured. All with too many expletives to count. I mean I'm no intellectual myself but I got bored smiling politely at the thirty-fifth telling of what a shotgun blast does to a stomach at ten feet. Or then you had the first-timers to Spain, complaining about everything: it's too hot, it's too expensive, don't understand the menus… blah fucking blah. Add to that most of the girls that hung out were mostly either spoilt little rich kids, pasty tourists or beauties removed of cerebral capacity.

Yeah, Toni at least had something to say. She

talked about art and food, where she'd live, childhood memories even politics.

She was around for another of those memorable days of my life. It's like I said, lots of things seem to have a pivot point. I didn't know at the time that Johnny was about to step up Tom's contribution to the Johnny Fay retirement fund. It certainly was a busy day for Johnny, but at least I got out into the sun. And I had a chat with Toni.

I had dropped Johnny off at Juan's office in the early morning and took a leisurely breakfast. It was in Málaga. You know most people look at Málaga as just another big Spanish city with some nice architecture but it's actually one of the oldest cities in the world – about 2,800 years old founded by the Phoenicians about 770 BC. I loved it as long as I steered clear of the tourist traps.

Besides it meant I had something better to do than sit in at Johnny's meeting. The less I seemed to know, the better, but I wasn't stupid either. I knew exactly who was there: Mark, Juan, Oliver and Johnny at the head of the table.

Johnny would take a sheaf of papers from Oliver and scan them. Oliver would tell him that after the business deals there was a hundred thousand pounds already in from Tom's apartment deal and another fifty thousand from Saul's villa. The lot of them would salivate at the thought of more cash at least ten grand each with the balance going to Johnny's account.

He'd also be lining them up for new scores, new marks and new deals. He'd probably have been getting the latest update on Kenneth Noye's Atlanterra home from Mark, how Oliver was handling some of Tom's accounts as he transferred more cash from the UK to Spain and Switzerland. Knowing Johnny, he promised more business to come and that they should "trust him". They'd already made a load of cash over the past ten years from his 'ideas', so they would trust him.

I know one thing, it was the meeting when Johnny laid down the law on property purchases – anything bought through him had to have him on the deeds, whether the real owner knew it or not and that was always not. Juan's expertise handled that. Anything except Kenny's little deal, of course.

You don't fuck mates over, after all.

Business didn't take that long and I picked up Johnny to take him to meet Toni for lunch. It turned out that she was heading back to Italy sometime in the afternoon. "Family business with her grandfather" was what she'd told Johnny when organising the date.

We picked Toni up from a new hotel not far from the seafront called Vincci Selección Posada del Patio hotel. It was in a great position to walk to most of the decent sites in Málaga, just on the Pasillo Santa Isabel. Two old four storey buildings had been renovated into one, its ochre coloured walls homing over a hundred rooms.

Toni had leaned through the open driver's window and gave me a peck on the cheek when she came out of the hotel and then turned to Johnny, hugged him and jumped in the back of the Range Rover. Johnny got in beside her.

"I just love that hotel," she said breathlessly. "Sitting up on the roof in the pool at night looking at the lit up church towers and the candles on the dark hardwood floors, it's dreamy."

I could see Johnny smiling at her. "I like those ruins of the Roman and Arabic city under the glass floor in the bar area," I answered.

"Yeah okay Bill," said Johnny "Remember it's the Maricuchi restaurant out at Pedregalejo beach. I hope you love your seafood, Toni, platters of prawns and sardines on skewers," speaking more softly to her.

"It's a shame you can't come boat-hunting with me later this afternoon," he continued.

"Yes, I'd have liked that but I have to catch this flight this afternoon – my grandfather's not too well and wants to see me," said Toni in a slightly sad tone of voice.

"How long will you be away? Not long, I hope. Oh, sorry again. That was very rude and inconsiderate of me," apologised Johnny rapidly. "I didn't mean anything bad about your grandfather."

But she was gentle again in her reply. "No. You're okay. I'm afraid it'll be as long as it takes, but I can still phone you and you me."

That's when he said it. Johnny said "I'll miss you Toni, so much."

Blimey, I thought, I hadn't heard him sound that sincere since pleaded 'Not guilty' to the charges of living off of immoral earnings.

I drove down Calle Bolivia and then turned right into the narrow Calle Varadero, a dead end. I have to admit the area didn't look great and at other times of my life if someone had driven me down a street like this the hairs on the back of my neck would be standing up. But I also knew the restaurant, the food was superb, it was right on the beach and if you knew the owner, the service was good.

I pulled into the car park let them out and left them to their tête a tête lunch.

Johnny had a very boozy lunch; I could tell by the glaze on his eyes. Toni had left for the airport by taxi and told him not to come with her. But after half an hour of driving back to Estepona with Johnny in silence, somewhere between drunken apathy and teenage angst, he physically shook himself, turned to me and said, "Right Bill we've got some business to do, selling a very expensive yacht." he smiled at the thought of it. Then he said, "It might just keep the fucker out of the club."

I understood "the fucker" was Tom.

It was somewhere around half past five when we met Tom and the ever-present Tracy at the Estepona Marina. The shops and bars were busy around it as tourists wandered the five minutes from the old town to see how the other half lived. It sported some of the most expensive and stylish private craft money could buy.

And we'd brought Tom to look at one of them.

It was moored at the premier site in the Marina, not along the crowded jetties, but outside the what I called the Tower. Like so many of the other buildings around the end of the marina, it was painted white and sea blue. But this one had four storeys in ever-decreasing size of hexagonal floors. Each floor had its own castellated patio. The marina had certainly developed far more seductively than I would have thought all those years ago when I watched from here as Johnny came in with a load of very profitable coke bouncing in the semi-rigid inflatables, dawn just broken.

We walked under the palm trees down the esplanade, Johnny chattering away, Tom clutching Tracy's hand.

There she was, announced Johnny with a flourish of arms. Tracy squealed. Tom whistled. It was called The Good Hope. Even I thought it was a beauty – An 88 feet long, Admiral motor yacht with a fly bridge, raised pilot house and aluminium hull and superstructure. I knew something about boats after all the years out here and even I knew this would be a costly purchase.

"Welcome aboard," said a man at the top of the gangplank. "My name's Piers, I'm here to show you the joys of this masterpiece of marine engineering." He had a broad South African accent, sun-brown skin and a smile like an alligator. He had blue sailing shoes, white chinos with a small brown leather belt and a sea blue polo shirt. He had a pair of aviator glasses perched on the top of his short dark hair.

Johnny snorted and said, "I expect the boat to live up to the patter, matey-boy."

"I'm sure it will… mister?"

"My name's Johnny Fay, this is your interested party, Tom and his lady-friend Tracy," he replied, smiling and gesturing to his special guests. "This is Bill my associate."

"Ah yes Mr Fay. Please, all of you feel free to wander around then come back to me and I will explain it all."

It was certainly some boat. The decks were laid with teak. At the top was a fly bridge with a sofa for three persons in white faux-leather sitting at right angles to the pilot's seat, dashboard, wheel and throttles. The back of the deck had chrome handrails, a high-tech radar dome and canopy to be raised when the sun become too unbearable.

Down the steps you could either enter the tinted double glass doors to the saloon or head out to the aft deck, dark teak flooring, sofas and tables and gate access to the aft dive platform.

Below was the covered pilots position and saloon, black tinted windows to give privacy to the sofas that surrounded the walls and the home cinema system. Beyond that was an independent dining room with table for eight guests. Bedding them was easy too. The master stateroom was midships with a walk-in wardrobe, TV, satellite link-up and a en-suite bathroom. The wood work was done in light ash and the tiling with plain white and blue ceramics, as it was throughout the boat. Forward was a VIP stateroom with walk-in wardrobe and en-suite. There was a guest stateroom port side, with twin lower beds and a Pullman berth, also with an en-suite bathroom. The starboard side had a similar guest room.

Through the galley and down steps lay the three crew cabins berthing five and a bathroom.

I could see that Tom was more interested in the toys and look rather than any practicalities, just as Johnny thought. Johnny certainly egged him on about the GPS/Plotter/Radar Simrad CX54 Navstation in pilot house, or the Philips Navigator, or the Geonav Elite on the flybridge, or the depth sounder or the VHF radio systems. Even the button marked 'anchor' fascinated him.

"Well it beats the crap out of a bloody ambulance," enthused Tom, to all that could hear, as he sat himself in the pilot's seat.

Personally I'd heard enough after fifteen minutes. But not Piers and Tom. I'd been on loads of boats and enjoyed them but never saw the point of owning one. If you wanted one, rent it by the day or week. These things were like pouring money into a deep-sea whirlpool if you owned it. After nearly an hour of looking in cupboards, at engines and generators and control systems and pumps, Piers eventually beckoned for Johnny and Tom to join him on the aft deck at a table.

Johnny nodded to me to keep Tracy sweet. I lead her past the day toilet and shower on the side deck and along to the forward sunbathing deck, complete with its own bench fridge and drinks cabinet.

Every now and again I could catch part of the conversation on the breeze and while I was facing Tracy, chatting amiably, I could also see the three at the table talking intently.

"So how much is it Piers?" asked Tom.

"In sterling it's £750,000, Mr Papworth," replied Piers without flinching. Before Tom could say anything in return Piers turned to Johnny and said, "By the way Mr Fay, Mark Lufton asked me to tell you that he has found a small marina operation up for sale at a million Euro, should you be interested." He smiled at Johnny.

"Interesting," said Johnny slowly. He looked over at Tom, "Well at least then you'd be spared mooring charges for this beast, wouldn't you Tom?" This time Johnny smiled at Tom.

Tom laughed. "That'd be good of you."

Johnny's face became more serious but in a soft way. "No seriously Tom, we could go into business together, you and me. I know you're interested in boats and with a marina, you could run the business. I'd look at it as an investment and we could use my contacts to expand."

"What? You'd be my partner in a business? A boat business? Yeah. No problem." Tom turned to Piers and added, "I'll take the boat and me and my new partner will look at the details and outlines of the marina too." He held out his hand and shook Piers' vigorously, while Johnny leaned over and slapped Tom on the shoulder. "Nice one Tom, it's a wise move for both of us and a nice little earner. Go and tell Tracy."

I could see Tom leaving the huddle and coming my way. I got up and started to wander back to Johnny. He had turned to Piers. "You can get in touch with Juan. He'll deal with all the legals and Oliver will deal with the financial stuff from the bank. I take it you understand what's expected," said Johnny, tilting his head to one side and pausing.

"Mark has told me about the operation," replied Piers with a brief nod and a smile to Johnny.

"Well I think that's us done for now," said Johnny as he got up and walked towards me and Tom.

"Well now Tom, Piers will sort out the paperwork for you, and Juan and Oliver are ready to do all the niceties for you. Me and Bill have to get back to the club. See you later?" said Johnny amiably.

"Nice purchase, Tom," I congratulated him, with a slap on the back.

But that wasn't the end of our day.

Tom turned up at the club at about eleven o'clock. We weren't too busy. A few of the regulars were there, Big Harry, Tosh, Slasher Sam and Frankie the Fright. They were all exiles from Blighty and they missed it.

Most nights of the week they sat at the booth inside the front doors, right next to the open windows. They read the British papers, complained about the state of Britain and what immigrants had done to England. They also played cards. You name a game, they played it – even Bridge. And they gambled on everything, all the time. It seemed to be the only way they could keep their sanity.

There were a couple of tables of youngsters out on the terrace, chatting, laughing and flirting. There were also four or five tables of tourists eating a late dinner.

Roberto was running bar. I was sitting at the end of it in my usual position when Tom came in with Tracy. I was expecting him to be over the moon with having bought The Good Hope. It took a lot to get Tom down. He came straight over to me and ordered a whiskey and glass of house white for Tracy.

He gestured to me but I turned the offer down. "What's the matter with you? You couldn't get that huge smile off your face a few hours ago," I said. I could tell he'd been drinking. Before he could tell me, Johnny wandered out of the office and came over. I looked at him and nodded towards Tom.

"Why the face, Tom? I thought you were happy with that beauty and our future business?" said Johnny looking concerned.

"Aww Johnny it's not that. I had a call from the ex-wife, telling me her new boyfriend has been violent with her and shouting at the kids. I know we're not together but I've still got a loyalty to her and worry about the children. You know how it is," Tom said plaintively. I was still thinking about Tom's statement – loyalty, "you know how it is" – that was one thing Johnny Fay didn't know.

Johnny glanced at me. Then he turned to Tom and looked seriously at him. "So, what do you want to do then Tom? I mean this is serious."

"I'd like to go and get violent with him," said Tom bitterly, alcohol boosting his bravado.

It was like watching a devil. It was as if I was the only one who could see the real Johnny. He wasn't leaning forward on the bar listening intently to Tom, he was really standing behind him pulling strings, whispering in his ear, reading his thoughts, reading him like a book.

"You have money Tom. Why get your hands dirty?" Johnny whispered.

Tom paused and looked directly at Johnny. "What do you mean? Pay someone?" he replied croaking.

"Well, yes. Pay someone else to do it."

"I, I mean, I wouldn't know where to start... who to ask," Tom stuttered.

Johnny intercepted. "Don't worry, I'll make a call later. Now cheer up you old bastard, will you? I can't have a partner down in the dumps. You have to celebrate your boat. Here Bill, get a bottle of bubbly. I have some more work to finish up and a couple of calls but I'll be out soon."

I called Roberto over and ordered the silver service.

Johnny wouldn't mind the bill, it would come under expenses. By this time Tom seemed to be getting back to his old self, pulling Tracy into his hip and giving her a peck on the cheek.

A big group of tourists had turned up by the time Johnny came back to the bar from the office. He whispered in Tom's ear, "Tom. Get rid of Tracy for a minute, leave her with Bill. I need to talk to you urgently."

Tom turned to Tracy and said, "Listen love I've got have a quick chat with Johnny. You know, business. Go have a chat to Bill."

Johnny led Tom away from the bar to the back of the club, under the sweeping black drapes and trellis wall. There was no one at the club's rear, it was an area for staff only with Johnny's office, a staff room, kitchens and stores. He grasped Tom's arm and gently pulled him towards him.

"What is it mate? What's happening?" asked Tom quietly.

"Look I made a phone call. I have some boys lined up and ready to go. Now the thing is they wanted thirty thousand pounds. You know an arm, a leg or two and a clear message. Just let him know, yeah?" whispered Johnny.

Johnny knew the bottle of champagne would make Tom feel even more brave than an hour ago. Tom simply nodded and smiled to himself. He then walked back to the bar and ordered another bottle of champagne.

Johnny rubbed his hands together and returned to his office.

I thought that was the end of an active day. I wanted to get home but there were still of fair number of good spending regulars. Harry, Tosh, Sam and Frankie were still playing cards and drinking lager. The tables outside still had people drinking. And quite a few tourists came in and out. There was obviously a few tour buses in town and dribs and drabs of their passengers constantly drifted from one bar to another.

I suppose it was strictly the next day when it happened. About 1 a.m. Another bunch of tourists had drifted in, mostly girls but seconds after in came three blokes in their early thirties. They'd followed the girls. I sussed them immediately. When you've been in the bar game for any length of time you can smell trouble and trouble makers. Maybe its testosterone or some hormone, but you can literally smell it.

The three of them had Arsenal football shirts, skinheads, white legs and tattoos. Fucking tattoos. I was ashamed of Britain. You could always tell a Brit, he or she was the one with the tattoos everywhere. It's like at some point someone put a tattoo virus in the water. The Germans didn't do it, nor the Italians, the Spanish, the Moroccans, only the Brits. And I wasn't talking about the old school, like Frankie or Sam. That was a prison thing, boredom relief.

But it was like Tom was a magnet. They picked up the three bottles of lager from one of the female bar staff. One of the men, it was hard to tell one from the other – not a strand of hair on any one of them, nudged his mate and gestured towards Tom. Noticeably the group of girls collected themselves and slipped out the doors, seeing the Arsenal crew were preoccupied.

Tom was oblivious to them, too involved in talking to Tracy. God knows what they found to talk about. She was nice enough, knew when to keep quiet and give Tom some space. She liked reading and could sit for hours while Tom drank and she just read. But she could also be good fun telling risqué jokes. She was a divorcee I think, all paid for in Spain and a flat in London, but probably bored. And let's be honest, Tom was genuinely a nice bloke. He had funny stories about the ambulance service – the old dears who collapsed trying to get to the hospital by walking, while the big Asian families who had six cars in the drive decided they needed a 999 call because Auntie had a sore toe. No one cold possibly take them in a car. He'd had enough of that crap.

They'd obviously copped who Tom was. I couldn't believe that any of them could read, but I knew it'd be trouble, especially in the mood Tom was already in. Before I heard the first "Ain't you that Tom bloke, the fella that drove the ambulance and won over six million quid?", I had started calling Johnny from the office. Roberto had already spotted my worries and moved down the bar towards Tom.

"Come, quick Johnny. I think you'd better get out

the front, trouble's following Tom. It could get nasty, mate," I said.

The next thing I knew was Johnny walking to the end of the bar. By this stage, the curious banter had become decidedly more aggressive, especially since Tom had uncharacteristically asked them to leave him alone when they'd demanded drinks. I saw Frankie and the boys look up from their cards. They clocked Johnny's look of anger.

One of the idiots had got hold of Tracy's arm, not hurting her exactly, but stopping her from doing what she wanted. Tom might have wanted to do something but one of the other Gunner's fans had pinned Tom by the neck to the bar. He was threatening to smash his beer glass in his face, screaming, "Well give us some money then Mr Tom the millionaire. Sit there and ignore us just because you think you have money and so you're better then us? I don't fucking think so."

Parts of the bar had gone quiet. None of the tables sitting outside knew anything was going on but I had noticed that Big Harry, Tosh, Slasher Sam and Frankie the Fright had got quietly up from their card game. Frankie and Sam had gone to the front doors, closed and locked them. Harry and Tosh stood close by, all four watching me, Johnny and our "guests".

Roberto had nodded to two of the other male bar staff who had slipped out to cover the back exits.

"Well, well, got a couple of big boys here have we?" said Johnny loudly. For those customers who hadn't heard the yobbos shouting initially, Johnny's dramatic statement made them look up. He had moved from the staff entrance flap slowly round to where Tom was at the bar. Myself and Roberto moved in from the other side.

The bloke who had Tom by the neck looked over at Johnny. "Well what the fuck does Granddad want then?"

"Funny boy. My friends and me," said Johnny nodding at the London contingent already standing by the front door, "... don't like people like you." As the lads chanced a glance at Frankie, Sam and Co, Johnny brought up a lightweight baseball bat from where it had been hidden by his leg and swung.

The bloke who was holding Tom was just returning his gaze to Johnny when the end of the bat made contact with his jaw.

I love movies and this was one scene that reminded me of a Sam Peckinpah western, where violence erupts and it all goes into slow motion. The bat made one hell of a crack and the bottom of the guy's jaw moved faster than the top, a millisecond pause and a string of blood flew over Tom's head and across the bar. It was followed by what must have been teeth. He then hit the deck.

The other two, weren't quite in range but were now caught with the boys at the door, Roberto and me on one side and a very angry Johnny twirling a baseball bat like a Majorette. "You want some of this as well? Well do you?"

By this time a frozen Tracy had pulled away from the guy holding her arm and moved to Tom's side. "You bastards. Get off him," and put her arm around his shoulder.

The bloke who'd met Johnny's baseball bat was groaning, his 'mates' unsure what to do next. Johnny nodded at me. "C'mon you two cunt's get your mate up and fuck off," I said.

Johnny pointed the bat at them as they dragged their moaning friend halfway to his feet, "You two – fuck off out of my club. If I ever see you here again I will fucking kill you. Don't you ever show up on my turf again. Now get out."

I turned around and signalled for some bright music to be pumped in. The murmur of voices began again. Frankie, Sam, Harry and Tosh were already back at their cards, door unlocked. Johnny signalled Roberto for a bottle of whiskey to go to the London contingent.

Tracy was whispering over a shaken Tom, "You alright darling? Those bastards."

"Yeah, love, I'm fine. Thank's Johnny. You're just like my older brother: always there when I need you," he croaked.

"I told you Tom. If you're with me nobody fucks with you, because they will be fucking with me, it's the way it works," Johnny laughed.

Tracy dragged Tom to the dance floor to take his mind off of what just happened.

"They started because Tom refused to buy them a drink, that's all. They definitely recognised him when they came in," I said.

"They couldn't just take a drink and enjoy themselves. Keep an eye on him, for fuck sake Bill. I don't want anything to happen to him just yet," whispered Johnny.

Because of the night's events, I got around to Johnny's villa early. Tom was there, he'd ended up staying the night.

Myself and Tom were eating a hearty and healthy breakfast in Johnny's arched patio area. The sun was already blistering hot so the fresh fruit and jugs of orange juice were making life more bearable.

Johnny came down the steps from the house and pulled up a chair. I glanced at him and nodded towards Tom.

"So how're you doing this morning then, Tom?"

"Ah okay, Johnny. Morning hangover from last night. Listen. I've been thinking about last night. What you said, you know at the beginning of the evening."

Johnny glanced at me and asked, "What was that, then?"

"Those people from London, Jon. You know the ex's boyfriend thing."

"Yeah, well what about them?" answered Johnny a little impatiently.

Tom looked at me nervously then looked back to

Johnny and then dropped his voice. "After last night, I really don't want him hurt badly. The missus rang to tell me they've made up."

"Are You sure? I mean those lads are probably on their way by now or at least been given the job. Look, let me make a call," said Johnny soothingly. He got up from the table winked at me and disappeared into his office in the tower. That left me to pass small-talk with Tom, mostly about his boat.

In less than five minutes Johnny was back. "Look Tom, they've already been contracted and are heading out right now. The issue is that at this stage of the game that if the job is cancelled, they will do to you what they were going to do to him. Sorry mate that's the way it works unless you pay them something," explained Johnny sympathetically.

I sneaked a look at Tom. He looked as ill as he had in the club last night when his face was kissing the bar top. He was rubbing his hands. "Can you pay them? What do I need to pay them? Just pay them Johnny, please," he asked plaintively.

Johnny smiled. "Look don't worry. You were going to pay them thirty grand, just pay them ten thousand to cancel. That'll keep them happy. Call it expenses. I'll make the call and will make the relevant transfers."

"Alright Johnny I'll pay that. I can cope with it. I'll draw that out from the bank tomorrow. Are they open now? I'll check. Yeah, I'll head off Johnny and get my act together," said Tom almost panicking.

And with that and a few slamming doors and Tom was gone.

Johnny's face was red from holding in a series of guffaws that burst out when we heard Tom's car pulling out. I looked at Johnny smiling. "Okay, what is it? What's so funny?"

"Come on Bill you must have guessed. That's the quickest ten grand I've ever earned. Make a call he said, tell them not to come," he mimicked Tom and continued laughing.

"You never called anyone in the first place, did you, you bastard? You didn't, did you?" I asked, sniggering.

"Bingo, Bill. No. No, I never called in the 'boys' in the first place. Ten grand, lovely jubbly."

I had to admit Johnny could make anything earn a crust.

Chapter Nineteen
Goodbye Kenny

It had been a couple of weeks since Johnny had called Mr Elder. He'd gone out fishing with Bill one afternoon and it came to him that he couldn't resist watching Mr Elder flapping on a line for a while. It had made him laugh at the time but he had decided just to say "Nothing" when Bill asked what was going on.

All of Johnny's business with Kenny was long done. He'd helped with the paperwork and money-moving for Kenny to buy his new pad in Atlanterra. For that and making Kenny's life easier, he'd been paid another twenty thousand. Johnny doubted he'd see much of him over in Estepona. Kenny would be keeping low in the gated community using the bars and restaurants, the private beach and staying out of the way.

Except... Except, there was still always the seafood bar in Marbella that he went to once a week. The two of them had dined there several times and Kenny had boasted how he knew everything on the menu and always got the best view of the sunset. And Kenny was a man of habit.

Johnny figured the time was right to take the final payout from the Kenny Noye saga.

But that didn't mean that he couldn't still have a bit of a wind-up.

He had gone home, poured a drink, put his feet on

the desk and dialled Mr Elder's number. Before Johnny could say anything, Mr Elder immediately said "Hello, I hope you've got something for me Johnny-boy after this long wait."

"And nice to speak with you too, Mr Elder. As you may have guessed, I'm calling you about our mutual friend."

"Spit it out Johnny, what have you heard? Where's Noye?"

"Well you're right. I may have heard something about Kenny Noye. Problem is that I really can't say at the moment. However it will give you time to get the money together in cash. Remember seventy grand in sterling."

"Stop messing me around, Fay," shouted DI Elder but Johnny had already hung up. He also refused to answer the phone when DI Elder called his number back, only leaning over and switching it off.

Elder leaned back on his cheap office chair, thinking why was he still in the business, why didn't he retire? He could. Old Detective Chief Superintendent Farringdon had gone, not that Johnny Fay would know, he thought bitterly. He was still a Detective Inspector, in spite of all the interesting jobs he was given.

Old Farringdon – he'd liked working with him. Maybe because it wasn't all the time, or maybe because the cases were generally interesting. All that inter-agency stuff. He had learned a lot from him and patience was the key. Sure Noye had got off the Fordham thing.

Sure, he was regarded as the force's worst nightmare, but his time would come. That was the Farringdon rule, patience, that and play devious.

Sure he hated dealing with scum like Joe Wilkins, but he hated Kenny Noye even more. Joe's time would come too, he was sure of it. Thanks Mr Farringdon, you made me feel better, he thought.

Johnny's second call was a week or so later. DI Elder had been preparing a few of the participants. The red top newspaper editor had been fine about coughing up £50,000, so long as his paper got a scoop on the nicking of Noye. Especially a good picture. That didn't cause DI Elder any problems, in fact the thought of Kenneth Noye splattered across the national press, head hung low, hands in cuffs, appealed to him. The family of Stephen Cameron were desperate to see Noye pay for his crimes and Elder found little resistance in getting the further £20,000.

"Hello Jon, hope you're not going to hang up on me again," he said quietly.

"Yeah sorry about that. Just wanted you to realise the seriousness of this deal. Noye uses a particular local restaurant along the Costa del Sol on a particular day. I will tell you the time and day and name of the restaurant, when you give me the cash," said Johnny firmly.

"Well just make sure the day of our meet is the day of Kenny's dinner engagement," said Mr Elder. "It'll take me two to three weeks to get the paper work finished and then there's the cooperation of the police out there."

"Sure, sure, I know the drill. When you're ready, call me," concluded Johnny, putting down the phone.

Three weeks later Johnny was sitting in his Range Rover outside Málaga Airport, with the sun nearly at its zenith. He was in a layby not far from the main gate, air-con left running. Johnny was reflecting on how Kenny was going to react tonight and what he was going to do with the £70,000 he'd earned or was about to.

His daydreaming was interrupted when a large black four-wheel drive Mercedes drew up beside him. It was one of those new Mercedes ML320s. He'd just seen them on Spielberg's Jurassic Park follow up 'The Lost World'. It was high and wide and although the Germans were aiming to take on the Range Rover with this model, he reckoned it was a pile of shit. I mean it looked like a Panzer Tank and only had an automatic gearbox which he believed was useless for a four-wheel drive.

Its tinted passenger window buzzed downwards and there was DI Elder, big smile on his face. In the driver's seat was certainly another of the Met's finest. Nothing for style or the temperature, thought Johnny. DI Elder on the other hand, actually had a casual open-necked shirt and light jacket.

Johnny lowered his own window and smiled. "I see you've been getting fashion lessons, Mr Elder. It's nice for me to be waiting at the airport for you rather than the other way around. 'Bout time if you ask me," said Johnny.

"Always the smart chat, now where's MacFadden? Left him at home? Fallen out?" Elder shrewdly asked.

"He's out of this one Mr Elder. But I do know he'd approve of your motor. He never stopped moaning about your preoccupation for brown Granada's. Now are we ready to finalise our arrangement?"

"Listen Johnny, you'd better not be pissing me about. After that little Danny Boy mess and not clearing off after the first time you walked out on Her Majesty's hospitality, you've used up a lot of your lives with us. There'll be no spending that cash if I don't come home with Kenny," warned DI Elder. He paused for effect. "I've got the heavy mob following and they're chomping at the bit."

"Well pass me the cash then and let's get on with it," said Johnny, curtly. Elder reached between his legs and pulled up a brown leather doctor's bag. He passed it through his window and into Johnny's welcoming arms. Elder noticed that Johnny immediately checked the contents, flicking through each cash pile. He wouldn't be surprised if Johnny Fay could actually count that fast too, he was one greedy bastard.

Johnny put the bag into the passenger seat footwell and turned back to DI Elder. "Okay Mr Elder, we're heading to Marbella. Follow me and keep your phone switched on," said Johnny.

He led the Mercedes west down the AP-7, through

Torremolinos and past a generally brown landscape of scrub land, interrupted by olive groves and vineyards. Often the deep motorway cuttings hid any countryside at all. It took Johnny less than forty minutes to get to where he wanted.

By this stage he had collected a proper convoy. His Range Rover. DI Elder's Mercedes, a battered BMW, a Ford Transit panel van and a couple of patrol cars.

He pulled into a quiet neighbourhood along the Calle Carril del Relojero in Elviria, Marbella. Everything pulled in behind him and DI Elder got out of his vehicle and wandered up to Johnny's window. "Okay Johnny, where the fuck are we?"

"Don't your Spanish mates know? Okay, okay can't blame a man for having a little fun, eh? See that next left, well you go to the bottom – it's a dead end to the beach – and there's small car park. To one side is a seafood restaurant. Kenny loves the place, he'll be there," explained Johnny. "He's most likely sitting on the terrace, closest to the beach."

Elder said nothing but turned around and walked back to the BMW. After a minute or so he straightened up and walked back to Johnny's car. The BMW pulled out leaving DI Elder and Johnny looking through a fine haze of dust. It turned left.

Johnny felt unnerved by Mr Elder's silence. He was just standing, waiting by Johnny's window. Johnny nearly jumped when DI Elder's mobile phone rang. It was one of the two undercover police officers from the

BMW. "Ah Señor Elder, we are in luck, I can see him at a table facing the beach under the canopy."

"Okay, we know what to do. Be there with the boys," answered Elder before hanging up. "Nice work Johnny. Now you'd better clear off while we go to work. I do love my job sometimes. By the way how old do you think you'll get to Johnny? Everyone runs out of luck."

"Yeah well I make my own luck. Go get your man, Mr Elder," said Johnny as he started the car and squealed away.

Ten minutes later Mr Elder appeared around the corner of the restaurant to the area under canopy. There was a loud murmur of surprised voices. A few English accents were disapproving but out of it all was Kenny's voice shouting, "Nah, fucking take it easy you stupid cunt. You've got the wrong fella'. This is a bit over the top."

The terrace was covered with a yellow waterproof material billowing gently in the beach breeze which pushed the waves Elder could hear rushing the shore. Several tables had been knocked over, their linen white tablecloths with decorative candles scattered amongst the plastic chairs.

Mr Elder looked down on Kenneth Noye as he lay prostrate on the patio's stained wooden floor. The two cops from the BMW were sitting with their knees in Kenny's back, holding his cuffed hands directly out from his back. Around them were another four Spanish policemen, side-arms drawn and pointed at Kenny, wearing black flak jackets with Policia across the front and back, their police identification badges hanging from a chain from their necks.

"Now, now Kenny. Me thinks you do protest too much. What with your track record and fascination for knives, I told them that if you even reached for a teaspoon they were to kill you," said DI Elder in a precise determined voice.

Kenneth Noye looked up at DI Elder's smirk. His face had changed from defiance, to shock but before any blood could whiten it, his veins started bulging. His red rage sputtered a question, "You. How did you know where I was? Who grassed me? You fucking pig. I asked who grassed me?"

"We've been looking for you, son. You ain't going anywhere on your own again for a very long time. I've been waiting to say this for quite some time, Mr Kenneth Noye, you're nicked, you fucking animal."

Chapter Twenty
Toni Returns

It was less than a week after our profitable 24 hours with Tom that Johnny called me into the office. He was looking shifty. Well that's to say as far as I was concerned Johnny always looked shifty even when he looked angelic. But today he was wriggling around in his chair.

"Okay Johnny what's up? Spit it out," I asked jovially.

"I've got a favour to ask mate. With this marina deal coming together, Tom's constantly at the villa again. Toni is coming back later and I don't want to go home and have silly bollocks hanging around. So… can I borrow your apartment for a few days while she's here?" the last few words tumbled out. I couldn't remember the last time I saw Johnny Fay embarrassed.

"Silly bollocks? Oh Tom. And I stay at yours?"

"Of course. You can stay there…"

"Right," I interrupted, "You mean I get to spend time with silly bollocks? Okay only joking. Look I'll go pick up some of my clobber and take some of yours over to mine, I'll shift some shit around. I already have my room at yours, so no problem, Johnny."

I headed off to sort out my apartment and pick up some of Johnny's kit. By the time I returned to the club it was evening and I was hungry. As I left my car I could see Johnny standing outside the club, in the outdoor patio area. He was standing under the trellis archway covered in Jasmine, smoking and looking up the street.

And then there she was. Even though the street was busy enough with people drifting around for drinks or dinner, Toni certainly stood out from the crowd – that easy, regal walk. She was wearing a cut long black dress with a light lamb's wool shawl – Colours of Benetton but more expensive, I thought.

I could see how many of the men were discretely stealing another look at this beauty as she walked past.

When Johnny spotted her, he quickly dropped his cigarette and stubbed it out. He waved. She returned it and smiled broadly. "Come back to me have you?" asked Johnny smiling.

"I couldn't stay away from my knight in shining armour, now could I?" she said as she reached forward cupped her hands around his cheeks and kissed him firmly on the lips.

"How was the family trip? Everyone well, I hope," said Johnny, as he gently herded her into the club.

For me it wasn't just another night in the bar. It was an opportunity to chat with Toni and get a breath of fresh air in my old lungs. Having said that I didn't want to become Johnny's third wheel and it sounded like this was the night he was going to make a move.

Roberto had been prepped and when Johnny had taken Toni to the end of the bar a glass of champagne

Son of Lucifer

had already been poured. He was whispering in her ear and she was giggling, not that girly giggle, that knowing womanly giggle. When she caught my eye me she waved and beckoned for me to come over.

"Hello Bill," said Johnny, as Toni put her arms around my neck and kissed me on the cheek. "Ah, hi Johnny. How are you Toni, have a good trip?" I stuttered. "Naturally darling, we must catch up soon," she purred.

I left Johnny and Toni to have a quiet meal in the dining area, candlelit and peaceful. I caught up on some paperwork in the office, the day's moving having disrupted the routine. Okay, I didn't have to move much in my apartment but there was enough to put away. There are a few photos of me and Johnny, an old black and white of my parents on their wedding day, faded and blurred but my one link with a family. I left those.

I liked art and had bought a few decent paintings over the years and a few knick-knacks that I knew would be a good long-term investment. But in terms of personal things, there was little in the apartment that said 'Welcome to Bill MacFadden's home'. It simply said 'Here's a lonely bachelor'. Even all my post went to the club.

By the time I came out of the office, Johnny and Toni had finished dinner and were sitting at the end of the bar. I overheard him tell Toni, that they'd make a move in about half an hour. He had to go and speak with Tom first.

When he turned around he saw me and said "Hi Bill, back in a minute, probably heading off though."

"That's okay. It still gives me a few minutes to chat with the delightful Toni," I said smiling.

Johnny said nothing but turned and walked off towards Tom's table. But Toni sparked up, "Oh Bill you trying to be even more gallant than my white knight? Let's chat, darling," putting her hand on my arm.

Johnny glanced backwards at us and continued over to Tom to tell him he was moving out but that I'd be there at the villa when he called.

As Johnny left for my apartment, he playfully punched me on the shoulder. "See you tomorrow, Bill."

Within half an hour Toni was leaning on the terrace's wrought iron balcony of my apartment. Partly in front she could see the winking lights of the Rock of Gibraltar. To her left, beyond the pool was the darkness of the Mediterranean. Behind her Johnny came from the living room through the double glass doors and across the solarium, past the sofas and coffee table and onto the marble patio.

"Making yourself at home? I'm afraid it's a bit of a bachelor pad but I am sure you will survive it." He handed her a sparkling drink. "Your vodka and tonic."

"I'm admiring your view. Close to the centre of town, right above the marina, views of Gibraltar and your own private pool on the roof. Your club is evidently an excellent investment," Toni observed. "You do very well for yourself," she added as she swept her hand across the view of what she thought was Johnny's apartment.

Toni had tried to peer into the darkness as Johnny drove her back from the club but hadn't seen the complex's name. They had pulled into an underground car park of a building that looked six or seven storeys, and by the signs there were five buildings in the luxurious complex. Semi-tropical plants were laid out with precision, communal gardens with fountains, walkways and promenades all observed by discrete security cameras. Not a stone out of place.

My apartment was one of four penthouses, and from what she could see it was probably the best one being a corner unit with uninterrupted views across the south coast and west to Gibraltar. No buildings to peer at.

The apartment itself was L shaped. The entrance gave a choice of corridor – straight on or to your right. It came to the living area. Modern, clean lines of the sofas and armchairs, a flat screen television framed on the wall, below it a dated Bang and Olufsen stereo. The room was about forty feet long and fifteen feet wide with the end of the room glass-walled and facing west, again in an L shape, also allowing you to sit on the sofa and admire the southward views.

Through the glass doors westward, was the wooden decking area for relaxing shaded by trellis. Through the south facing patio doors lay the marble roof terrace with a sun bathing area to the left and a raised swimming pool looking out into the infinity of the Mediterranean sea. Also looking onto the terrace was the dining room, open onto the Siemens-equipped kitchen and two of the three bedrooms, including the master, which had its own private access to another terrace.

The whole place stank of taste and money. It slightly surprised her. There was quite a selection of original artwork on the wall, most of it quite good, she thought. It wasn't sparsely furnished but it wasn't fussy either. Still, she thought, I was expecting to see a pool table or pinball machine somewhere in the place.

"Well I can't grumble," answered Johnny to her query of "doing all right". "Drink all right? Let's make ourselves comfortable."

Toni awoke before Johnny but she lay stock still. She needed to wait. She could hear his shallow breathing and as she watched a few whisps of cloud drift high across the sky, she could see above the pool. The odd bird drifts into view slowly becoming smaller as it used the increasing thermals to drift ever-higher.

She lay there for nearly an hour before she felt Johnny stir. She felt him swing his legs out of the bed and she quietly hugged the sheet to her breasts. He padded across the underfloor heated marble towards the en-suite and closed the door. Toni heard the shower flowing and after a pause when she assumed Johnny must be shaving, the door opened again.

Johnny slid a cupboard door open and pulled out a fresh shirt and pair of trousers. He opened a drawer beneath it and pulled out a pair of socks and boxer shorts.

Still Toni lay there until Johnny sat on the edge of the bed to pull his white Chinos on. She moved slightly then sat up, rubbing her eyes with the back of her hand, but keeping the sheet held high.

"Good morning sleepy head. Sleep well?" asked Johnny cheerfully. He leaned across the bed and kissed her gently on the cheek. "Look darling I have to go out and do a bit of business. How about we catch up later? Listen you take your time and let yourself out. There should be some breakfast in the fridge if you want it."

"Oh," said Toni sounding disappointed.

"Ah, don't worry we'll catch up later," said Johnny, leaving the bedroom.

Toni lay back down until she heard the front door close. She immediately got up and took a quick shower. After drying herself with a luxurious white fluffy towel, she wrapped it around herself and opened the bathroom cabinets. No doctor-prescribed drugs. Nothing personal at all.

She went back to the bedroom and slipped her clothes back on.

For the next thirty minute's she went through the apartment, starting with the main bedroom and living room. It was all so generic. There wasn't even paperwork. She had found a wall safe in the bedroom, but it required a digital key-code and that she didn't have. She wrote down the make and number.

She had certainly got a better look at the place and it was tasteful. While Johnny wasn't exactly a 'truffatore', a wide boy in English, she thought, his taste was practised rather than natural. No photo albums, she thought. A few pictures of Johnny with Bill and some black and white pictures. Toni's thoughts were interrupted by a key in the door and it opening.

An older woman dressed in a smart black uniform briefly startled when she saw Toni standing in the living room.

"Who are you? What do you want?" asked Toni.

"So sorry madam, I didn't know anyone would be here. I am here to clean apartment… So sorry to disturb you. I will come back in an hour only," the woman answered with a thick Spanish accent.

"No. Don't worry I'm just leaving." She picked up her handbag, took one last glance around the living room and left.

Johnny felt good about the day. It was going to be a profitable one, short term or long term. And the cherry on the cake was Toni. She was quite something. Or at least he thought she was. To be honest his memory was a bit shot. All that champagne and vodka, a few spliffs and a snort of powder he knew would make his memory hazy but, even so, he felt it was unusually so.

But Toni she was a tonic.

His mind had drifted back to her when Juan said, "This is fine with me. It's not too hard to do either." Johnny had to remind himself where he was. He was sitting at the head of the glass table in Juan's Málaga office conference room. But he had to glance up and grab a quick look to see who was there because he knew it wasn't the Winners. Mark Lufton was absent. Johnny remembered now, so far as he was concerned Mark had no role in this deal and was an unnecessary expense.

Juan sat to Johnny's left, Oliver to his right. Next to Oliver was a new face. Not new to Johnny, of course. Jason Richards. Jason 'Tricky Dicky' Richards was someone Johnny had known for many years. He was in his early fifties with a shock of grey hair at the front remaining dark at the back and a face wrinkled from laughing. Like Oliver and Juan, he wore a suit.

Oliver spoke next looking at Juan, "I can keep a distance on this, but still put the money through looking legal. The trail will disappear and I can still make official calls."

Johnny was back in action. "Ha, exactly what I want to hear. So it's a go then?"

Jason still hadn't spoken, but nodded his head with Juan and Oliver. Smiles all around then, thought Johnny. "I'll tell you when you're to make the call and the visit. All right Jason?"

Jason nodded again.

"Firstly, I'll set up a meeting with Saul and introduce you as the buyer, Jason. And remember, we've no personal connections at all. You only know of me through other people. We all know the procedure," said Johnny.

Just as he started to rise from his chair, he turned to Juan. "I take it all the details on the marina and boat have been finalised and sorted and Tom has his paperwork?"

"Si, Johnny. Everything was completed weeks ago. No problems," replied Juan.

They all solemnly shook hands and Johnny left them. Usually he would have stayed on for a tax-deductible lunch with Juan and Oliver, but it was a busy schedule. Next he had to see Saul, then meet up with Toni on Tom's boat.

Chapter Twenty-One
Temptation

An hour later Johnny was at Saul's villa. Not much had changed, although the garden looked like it could do with a little care and the windows seemed a little dirty. He rang the bell and within a few minutes he heard a gentle shuffle with some wheezing.

There was Maisie. I'm sure she's got thinner thought Johnny. He presented her with a bunch of flowers he'd bought at one of the service stations he'd stopped at on the way back from Málaga.

"Oh Johnny you shouldn't have. Thank you, please come in, Saul's by the pool. Go on out." Then Maisie raised her voice, "Saul it's Johnny, he's coming through." She coughed when she finished, a rasping, wheezing cough.

Johnny made his way to the back of the house, leaving Maisie to slowly make her way to the kitchen. It was nearly midday and Saul was sitting by a table with a sun canopy, a newspaper spread across the glass top.

Saul waved at Johnny as soon as he stepped out onto the pool terrace. "Yes, yes come and join me, Johnny. To what do I owe this pleasure?"

"Oh, it's just a quick visit. I've got some plans with a young lady later. Haven't seen much of you around lately, you and the little lady, all right are you?"

"We're fine Jon. Why do you ask?" By now Saul had become intrigued as to why Johnny was visiting.

"Well I was thinking of what you said to me soon after you moved in."

"And what was that Johnny?" asked Saul.

"Well you expressed concern as to whether your pension pot was big enough for this retirement, so I might have something to interest you, Saul," said Johnny slowly. Saul said nothing. "I have a buyer of diamonds who is coming to this neck of the woods for a few days. I'm doing a favour for a friend in London, you want to meet him?"

"But you know I'm not dealing any more, Jon," said Saul carefully.

"Look, Saul you can get credit, good credit. You sell to my man for the money, only we don't pay the VAT. You bring the stones over with you from your people in Tel Aviv," Johnny explained.

Saul listened quietly. Johnny thought he heard a little sigh before he said, "But that's smuggling Johnny. I don't know if I would be able to do this, I never have before."

Both men looked at each other intently. Johnny broke the silence. "We're talking about two hundred thousand pounds no risk profit, Saul." Johnny paused again, then noticed Maisie coming out with what looked like the lemonade tray. Oh no, he wanted a drink.

"Okay Saul think about it," as he got up from his

chair. "I have to be somewhere else in a minute, but think about what you could do with that kind of money."

As he turned he nearly bumped into Maisie. "Oh sorry darling, have to rush. Take care of yourself." He left.

Maisie looked confused for a moment. She put the tray down in front of Saul and then turned to watch Johnny disappearing into the shaded darkness of the house. "Saul why's Johnny going already? What's happening?" she said, a little concerned.

"Now, now Maisie calm yourself. He's a busy man, lots of deals to do. Sit down and join me for a drink of lemonade. Don't worry, rest yourself," said Saul calmly. He poured Maisie a glass of lemonade and then sat back stared into space and thought about what had been said to him.

Johnny had intended to head straight over to his and Tom's marina but the dealing with Saul had not gone as well as he'd hoped. He was beginning to find the old man annoying. Still it was just another iron in the fire. All that stress had his stomach rumbling so he stopped for a burger before catching up with the rest of them.

That meeting with Saul seemed to have made what started like an excellent day, go downhill fast. He felt removed from the rest of the day, even when he met Toni at the boat.

Since he and Tom had bought the marina (well at least that was what Tom thought) he'd seen much less of Tom. "Yet another upside," thought Johnny. Tom was actually turning the place into a good business. It wasn't as big as Estepona Marina by a long chalk, but it was easy to take yachts out of the water and into the yard for repair. The views from the sheltered bay and the small number of serviced jetties were second to none. It was amongst grass-covered stony hillocks with a solitary road winding up over the low hills to the rest of the Costa del Sol. There were several luxury villas on the hills' ridges and around the boat yard entrance itself were scattered picturesque cottages and cantinas.

He'd found Toni sitting at the back of The Good Hope with Bill. They had their backs to him as he walked along the pier and he could hear their laughing and the light tilting of heads while whispering conspiratorially and then giggling in unison.

There was some other flighty brunette that Bill had brought but he barely spoke to. Bill and his fucking bimbos, thought Johnny. There weren't many of them but he always managed to find them and bring them along at the wrong time. He'd been introduced to this one a few times but he still couldn't remember her name and found "Darling" adequate.

Tom was holding court in his usually good-natured way, making sure everyone had what they wanted. Tracy was there and like the other women, including Toni, was dressed in a challenging bikini. When Johnny thought of challenging is this respect, it wasn't so much challenging for the women to wear or look good in, but challenging for men to look at without drooling. My

Son of Lucifer

God, he'd thought old Pearl wore some revealing stuff back in the day, but now there was barely a centimetre left to the imagination. Toni was more conservative but nonetheless stunning in her one-piece bikini.

It was a usual afternoon on the boat. No one on board was sober enough to take The Good Hope out, but everyone was keen to drink. Johnny even provided a discrete snort down in the cabin, but he still didn't feel he was his sparkling self from this morning.

Bill had been entertaining the ladies for an hour with some card tricks he'd picked up over the years, while Johnny had been chatting with Tom about his plans for the marina. He didn't really care about the marina at the moment, he wanted to spend time with Toni, but she seemed oblivious to him and melted into the party crowd. Even when he'd taken his drink and wandered to the bow of the boat and looked out to sea and mull things over for ten minutes on his own, Toni hadn't joined him.

Even so he cheered up when at about seven, Toni walked up behind him, put her arms around his waist from behind and squeezed, "What's the matter my white knight, feeling that your armour is a little battered today? How about we go back to your apartment?"

In less than thirty minutes the two had made their excuses and Johnny opened the front door to Bill's apartment. He'd cheered up enormously with this more attentive Toni at his and no other wankers to talk to. "And at the moment that includes Bill," he thought.

"Hey darling, I've been buzzing around all day, I'm going to take half an hour in the bath and then we'll eat, is that okay?" asked Johnny. "Sure, I'm putting some music on," she said as she walked into the master bedroom. After she sorted the bedroom stereo, she lay on the bed still wearing the angelic-white one-piece bathing suit, a sarong wrapped around her waist, leaned on one arm and looked at Johnny.

"I'm going to rest here for five minutes or so, then change, so you get on with your relax time and then we have 'our' time," she purred.

Johnny disappeared into the bathroom turned on the taps and locked the door. Toni got up immediately and changed into a blouse with white trousers and threw her bikini and sarong into her large handbag. She listened at the bathroom door and could hear Johnny quietly humming to himself in the bath, the squeak of soap and the slosh of water.

Toni went straight to the bedroom closet where she had found the safe this morning. Johnny had been moaning about how hard a day it'd been for work. Well she'd been busy too. She'd made a few calls and learned something about this make of safe. So many hotel guests forgot their codes that each model had a permanent over-ride code, you just needed to know what to look for and add the appropriate digits.

She quietly slid the door open, knelt down and pulled back clothes to look under some folded collared polo shirts. She needlessly looked over her shoulder towards the bathroom door. Two minutes gone. She had memorised the number she was required to put into the safe and pressed the buttons quickly but carefully. The door popped open.

She looked inside memorising where everything was. There were wads of various currencies – Swiss Francs, Euros, Sterling and US Dollars. There was some jewellery, including some beautiful men's watches which she could never remember having seen Johnny wear before. There were some property documents. The only thing of interest was a leather-bound book.

Again she looked over her shoulder. A faint humming could still be heard. This time she also looked out towards the swimming pool through the patio doors. She turned her attention back to the book and unclasped it. A sheaf of little notes fell from the front and, as she balanced the book open to reinsert them, a little plastic packet fell from the back pages. Toni didn't notice it, instead concentrating on leafing through the book's pages. There were notes of places in London, what looked like accounts for the club or some club.

Then Toni heard a grunt and a splash. Johnny was getting out of the bath and could just walk in here in his robe, Toni thought.

She clasped the book and bundled it into the safe and closed it. She put the clothes back the way she found them. It was then she spotted the old bit of plastic wrapped around something. It had an embossed label. Toni looked back to the bedroom and decided to put the packet in her trousers. She got up and quietly headed into the living room.

She was standing by the window looking out at the view of Gibraltar in the hazy distance when Johnny walked in wearing a bathrobe and rubbing his thinning hair with a towel. In his other Hand he has his mobile and is finishing a conversation "… no problem. I'll see you tomorrow."

He looked up at Toni put the phone in his robe pocket and smiled. "You want a drink? Vodka?" he asked.

"Please. With tonic and ice."

Johnny walked to the small bar in the far corner of the living room and prepared the drinks. "Toni's quiet," he thought. He walked over towards her and put the clinking clear drink on the table next to her. He also put down a small wedge of Euros.

In silence. Toni glanced down at the money and then reached for her glass.

"Er, listen love. I've got some business to do tomorrow. How do you fancy going shopping with Tracy? There's some cash to get yourself something nice," he said.

Toni turned to Johnny fully face-on. Her normally bright angelic face, darkened. Her soft features hardened and her eyes peered into Johnny. "Don't patronize me. Who do you think I am? Some old English tart that hangs on your arm? The young Italian to do your catwalk?"

For the man that can read anyone, the outburst took Johnny-boy by surprise. It was the wrath with which the words were spoken, not their loudness or their profanity. "I don't understand, Toni. What is it? What's wrong?"

"I have warned you about doing this too often. I told you who I was the first time we met in Casares in the mountains. I told you what I expected, white knight. Do you think I am hard up for company or the good life? I have my own business, my own money, my own family, so fuck you Johnny Fay," she said with a fatal finality.

Toni ended her relationship with Johnny Fay by throwing the contents of her glass in his face. She marched past him, picking up her bag and stormed to the front door slamming it loudly.

Johnny wasn't going to take that in silence, flinging his own glass at the closing door and screaming, "And don't come back you whore. Go and find your soulmate, Bill. Bitch."

Son of Lucifer

Chapter Twenty-Two
Nearly an Eye For an Eye

I guess this was the day when I saw Johnny for what he really was. "And behold the beam was swept from the eye," or some such crap. Lucky it wasn't the eye, nearly though.

Looking back now, I suppose that anyone else might have thought I should have known better. I knew the moves, I had helped with many of them. By now it was 1999, twenty years after Dutch Benny had died. Nearly as long for Saeed. We'd got away with it. We hadn't seen Lenny Reed since that memorable night after our meeting with Carlos and Youssef.

We hadn't heard any more from Carlos or Youssef either. We were in the clear from all that – or so we thought.

As far as I was concerned, things were pottering along nicely. Deal here, deal there. Tom had coughed up a lot of cash, although he still didn't know it. I think Johnny still had some dealings with London. I know he had been talking to Mr Elder.

I suppose it was about six months after Kenny had been nicked. That stank of Johnny. I also know he'd not been around for most of that evening. I certainly remember because even though Ken was English mob, it made huge news over here. It was only another day before we had the British papers with Ken's mug all over them, as well. It became a bit of talking point around the bar for a week or so, but not a conversation that Johnny seemed to want to have. All he said to me when I told him the news was, "Shame. But I suppose that's the breaks."

I heard the car first. Myself and Johnny and Tempest, that's what she called herself, were lying by the pool. Myself and Johnny were dressed in shorts, both with short sleeved shirts completely unbuttoned. As much as I admire myself, I knew that we were nowhere near as desirably attired as Tempest. Another of Johnny's blonde "'playmates", her bikini bottoms which were nearly invisible and there was definitely no bikini top anyway. Perfect skin. Very relaxing.

I hadn't seen Johnny for a few days. He'd stayed out of the bar and sounded like a bear with a sore head when I spoke to him on the phone. He'd moved back to the villa but we'd missed each other. But him moving back to the villa told me that Toni wasn't around. I left it at that and when I turned up this morning to be introduced to the lovely Tempest, I figured it was better not to ask.

I got up when the swish of stones ended, went through the arches up the steps into the house and walked to the main doors. The bell rang. It was Saul. He'd been into the club a few times and said he'd come by to see Johnny. I hadn't expected him here. He gave me a hug. "Nice to see you Bill. Is Johnny here, can I see him?"

"Yeah he's here. Come on through to the pool," I replied. "How's Maisie?"

"Oh just as she was last week. But it's only time before it gets worse, thanks for asking, Bill."

Johnny had got up from his poolside seat and wandered into the arch room, with the bar and the long and well-used table. Tempest remained in unmoving worship of the sun – that poor body and skin wouldn't look so good in six years time.

By the time we came down the steps, Johnny was already pouring himself a drink. He looked up and smiled.

"Saul this is an unexpected surprise! How're you doing? What do you want to drink? 'Fraid I've no home-made cloudy lemonade," he said, laughing.

"I'll have whiskey please Johnny," Saul almost whispered. There was something about Johnny's demeanour. He was being his pleasant self but without his charm or faux-warmth. Maybe because he hadn't earned any more out of Saul over the past year. It was me that sat us down at the table.

We passed some small talk and Saul managed to tell a joke or two. Then he paused. "Jon, I know you remember the other day by the pool at my house when you told me you had diamond buyers? Do you still have that buyer's details?" His voice was almost hoarse. He took a deep slug from his whiskey.

Johnny looked up from his glass and peered at Saul. He ignored me. "What's happened to change your mind, Saul?"

I don't remember ever making the mistake before of involving myself in Johnny's negotiations, until I was given the nod, so to speak, but this time I answered Johnny first, "Look Johnny, Saul's wife is not…"

Again, as I'd seen before, his face seemed to change, just for a microsecond, then it became a glare, "Bill, I'm not fucking asking you. Go and ask Tempest to go home. Tell her I'll catch up with her later at the club, that this is urgent and quiet business."

I felt annoyed. That was out of order. I simply nodded, while Johnny turned his attention back to Saul. "Well Saul? What is the matter with the little woman, then?" asked Johnny sympathetically.

"Look, she's not well. I have to find some money to treat her properly, here. Does your man still want to deal?" asked Saul.

"Okay, I understand. I'll find out if he wants to buy at cost with us having the VAT, plus anything you can do on cost. How does that sound to you Saul?" asked Johnny.

I could hear the patter as I was walking over to Tempest and returned to the bar. She only shrugged, expertly wrapped herself in a sarong, put on her little bikini top, picked up her bag and left across the lawn, under, the arched wall into the drive and gone. But I'd still heard Johnny saying "How does that sound to you Saul?"

I wanted to scream "Don't Do It". It never ends well, I'd say. I knew he didn't want to do it, but over the past few months the old, jovial Saul had quietened down. He'd lost a little weight too. He was panicked with Maisie's illness – severe Alzheimer's Disease. She was going beyond the loss of memory and confusion. She was beginning to hallucinate, sometimes forgetting how to even use a fork. That homeliness had been all sucked out of her.

"Okay Johnny," sighed Saul. "Let me know, then I will set up a meeting with my man in Israel, negotiate a cost price and organise the credit line." He took a final sip from his glass, set it gently down on the table and got up slowly. He glanced over to me.

"Johnny, thank you. I must go now."

"Here why are you leaving? Have a drink with us, to celebrate us working together. You know you want to," pleaded Johnny.

"No I have to get back to my wife. She needs me. Goodbye," and he turned, nodded to me, and made his way through the house and back to the car.

I walked back to the table with my drink refreshed and another glass for Johnny. He was sitting staring into space, tapping his whiskey glass on his chin.

"Why'd Saul go?" I asked innocently.

"Dunno, said something about his wife, but I've got him on the diamond deal. Yes!"

"Look Johnny, his wife is really ill. She needs special treatment and you know how tight it is for Saul. Look at the state of him," I spoke quietly.

"Like I give a rat's arse about his old woman. Money. That's what drives me, Bill. You fucking know that," he sounded almost bitter.

"I've done a lot of things with you Jon, bad things and profitable things, but I can't do it to Saul. He ain't hurt me or you or anyone and he's in a bad place." Thinking back on it now I know that's what I said, but it never felt like it is was me speaking.

It was someone else. It was the bloke who was enjoying going fishing. The fella' fed up with endless hours in a nightclub with arse holes. It was the bloke who now had enough money to go where he wanted and simply enjoy life. Toni had told me a lot about Italy and while I'd been there a few times, I fancied the Bay of Naples, going to Sorrento and visiting Pompeii. I could even do it as part of a trip to the rugby World Cup in Australia, that was coming up in a few years.

I know all that went through my head but in that time I hadn't noticed that Johnny had got up from his chair across the table, picked up his drained whiskey glass and then it was a blur. I thought something had hit me along my cheek bone.

Nah, that couldn't be right.

But the next thing I knew is that I'm lying by the table and my chair is upended. I'm clutching my face and there's a salty, irony taste in my mouth. My tongue quickly checked to see if my teeth were still there and my lips. Okay. My hand feels sticky, but my face stings too. Then it hit me, the dregs of Johnny's whiskey was stinging pain to my cut face. But that means Johnny hit me with a glass. Me. Johnny. Glass in the face?

I felt sick. And then there was Johnny bending over me. "Johnny what're you doing for fuck sake? What's got into you Jon?" I said hoarsely.

It was then Lucifer spoke to me directly. "I have warned you many times, Bill. In London. In Morocco, even here in this villa. If you don't like what we do, then fuck off! Keep your mouth shut or I'll shut it for you."

He paused, then stood upright. He leaned forward again. "And, while we're at it, keep your fucking eyes off my girlfriends!"

He walked away and I heard his car screech out of the drive.

I just lay on the cool tiles, my blood masking their brown colour only darker. And the beam was swept from my eye. Fucking Joe Wilkins, Johnny Fay, my friend, my partner, my stupidity. Why was I surprised that he'd walk over me as he'd walked over everyone else?

Whoever heard of someone being a friend to Lucifer? Only a fool.

Son of Lucifer

Chapter Twenty-Three
More Pain

Another fucking night in this fucking, poxy nightclub. My face hurt and the painkillers didn't mix with the drink, as I'd found out last night. I couldn't even find the little bit of coke I'd stashed at home. I was sure I'd put it into my safe.

I'd dragged myself down to the hospital and got my cheek stitched up after the Johnny incident. We didn't talk for a few days. I didn't go into the club. I'd stayed away from everyone and hadn't spoken to Saul since that fateful afternoon or Tom either. I mean how was I meant to explain the big white patch on my throbbing face? Bee sting?

Yeah, my best mate glassed me. I felt humiliated. So that's what Johnny thinks of my opinion? After all these years running after him, easing the way, organising the nuts and bolts and keeping them greased.

I did a Johnny and brooded for a few days. I kept hearing the call of Gibraltar from the balcony but knew I was too boozed and drugged up to drive anywhere. I even thought about calling it a day in Spain and move on. But I liked the weather. And fuck Johnny.

I think it was about four days after the attack, that Johnny phoned me. He sounded sympathetic – "How are you Bill?" "I'm sorry, it was a bad day." "I had a lot on my mind." "Toni…" "When you coming back to the club?" I gave in. I agreed to come in.

He smiled when he saw me come into the club, "Look sorry Bill. How's the face, no permanent damage I hope," he said. Then it was back to normal. At least for him. It wasn't mentioned again.

A couple of months after that I was told to be 'on-duty', one of Johnny's contacts was coming to the club. Also Johnny had taken a phone call from Tom, who wanted to see him later. I was also there to run interference with him and Saul should it be needed. Yeah, I know, but Johnny said it was only a VAT scam and it'd make Saul some extra cash too.

I believed him, until Johnny's contact turned up. Fucking Tricky Dicky. I knew this wouldn't go well for Saul. Jason liked to describe himself as a grafter, but he wasn't like most of the grafters I knew. Most had some honour – leave old people alone. Go for the greedy, that sort of thing, but not this Jason Richards. He was a little shit.

But business was business, as Johnny liked to say so often. So like half of the rest of the regulars, I put up with him with a smile, bought a drink and laughed at his jokes.

Any way before Saul ever turned up Tom came in. No Tracy. "Must be serious," I thought.

Tom walked over to where Jason, myself and Johnny were standing. He glanced at the dressing on my face and looked as if he was going to ask the obvious, but Johnny interrupted him. "Hello Tom, to what do we owe the honour. Drink?"

"Er yes please. Just a whiskey, straight up," answered Tom. "Hi Bill, hello, er, Johnny I need to have a chat with you in private, if I can." "Sure, Look let me finish with Jason here, Bill take Tom through to the office. I'll bring your whiskey through, Tom," said Johnny.

I took Tom out the back to the office, unlocked the door and offered him a comfortable chair. "Johnny will be along in a minute, Tom. You look nervous, what's up?"

Tom said, "Do I? Well I hope Johnny won't get upset or take anything as an insult. I have something to ask him."

"Well ask straight out when he gets here," I said and turned to leave. The door opened and Johnny walked in holding Tom's drink.

I closed the door behind me, but didn't go back to the bar immediately. This sounded too interesting and something that might upset Johnny. Ha. It was Tom that spoke first. "Johnny I want you to understand this is not me being funny in any way with you, because you have been like a brother to me."

"That sounds ominous. What have you got on your mind Tom?" asked Johnny.

"It's the marina Jon. I've been doing all the work down there and I've built it up. I mean here's your share for this month."

"There's over 7000 Euros there Jon."

"And your point is what, Tom?"

I could hear heavy breathing now. Tom sure was nervous. "Well… I'd like… I'd like to make you an offer for your half of the business. I really like working down there. I like working with boats and going out on mine. It's my future."

I could almost hear Johnny smiling, "Not a problem Tom. I can do with a bit of cash flow for something else I am interested in. So come up with a price and we will talk."

"I'm really glad we got that sorted. I was so nervous about asking you," said Tom sounding relieved.

When Johnny informed him it was sorted and for Tom to go and enjoy himself, I made my way back to Jason. Tom looked happy when he waved as he left the club and moments later Johnny returned to the bar. He didn't look too happy. Not happy at all.

He managed to look cheerful when Saul wandered into the club about an hour later.

Saul looked quizzically at the dressing but again didn't ask any questions. Johnny spoke first. "Saul this is Jason. Jason this is Saul. I will take you both to the office and leave you to it. C'mon I have to get something out of my desk anyway."

I watched them all traipse off to the office and I stayed where I was. No need to run interference. Johnny came back with a small green canvas bag which he set on the bar in front of himself. "Roberto, get me a cup of coffee, por favor."

"Well apart from Tom's visit all seems to be going well. Listen does Tom spend every day at the marina and the office there?" Johnny asked me.

"Yeah. He likes to show off to that bird of his, Tracy. I mean it's a comfortable life."

"Okay, worth knowing. Listen I've a small job for you. Just drop this bag off at mine while I wait to see what is happening with these two. Take care," said Johnny.

"No problems, I'll see you tomorrow then," I said. Thank God, anywhere but the club and seeing Saul again. I went out to my car.

I got into my Land Rover Freelander and placed the bag on the seat next to me. I looked at it for what seemed like ages. Sod it. I unzipped the top of it. There was a package of coke, about half a 'key' I'd say. I recognised the red Rubber Duck Logo. But there was also a shooter, a US army issue 45 calibre Browning pistol.

What the fuck was Johnny up to this time?

Chapter Twenty-Four
Delicate Work

Fuck, it's hot, thought Johnny. He sighed to himself and thought, so what's new? He was waiting outside Málaga Airport. Again. He'd forgotten how many times he had flown in out of this place. How many times he'd waited for someone or dropped them off.

Suddenly he remembered waiting for Estelle nearly twenty years ago. Those terrible air hostess uniforms but that beautiful body. God how much had changed. She wouldn't recognise the airport, he thought. A few years after Estelle's visit, a new passenger terminal opened at the airport. Almost all arrivals now came here. On top of that the old passenger building was converted into a general aviation terminal, along with new hangars for maintenance and cargo.

He sighed to himself again. This time he was waiting for Saul. Not as profitable as Estelle's visit, but he could see some good money coming.

Unlike Estelle, Saul did not so much sweep out of the glass doors, than staggered. Already, even with an air-conditioned arrivals' room, Saul was wiping beads of sweat from his bald pate. He had a briefcase in one hand and a suit bag in the other, nearly hitting his own face as he mopped his brow.

Even so he was still wearing a grey Prince of Wales check Aquascutum suit. It was well made but Saul obviously didn't listen to the tailor who would have told him that a double-breasted cut didn't suit his rotund form. Black leather shoes, white shirt and blue tie set it off. Johnny shook his head. Saul certainly looked the part. It was certainly a case of you could take the Jew out of Hatton Garden, but you couldn't take Hatton Garden out of the Jew.

Johnny smiled broadly when he caught Saul's eye. Saul only nodded.

"Well Saul, good trip? Profitable, I hope?" Johnny queried enthusiastically.

"Everything went well," Saul replied briskly.

Johnny made a few non-committal comments as the two walked over to Johnny's parked Range Rover. He couldn't get as close to the terminal building as he had used to, but still closer than most. Half-way to the car Johnny stuck his hand out, "Here Saul let me carry that suit bag for you."

"Oh, yes please. Thank's Johnny," said Saul gratefully.

That's better, thought Johnny. Don't want Saul getting pissed off with me just yet. Still, Saul was unusually quiet.

Johnny threw the suit bag onto the back seat and climbed into the driver's seat. Saul climbed into passenger seat, now clutching the briefcase to his chest. The two paused and looked around.

Slowly, Saul opened his briefcase and took out a small wooden box. It was a dark wood, polished but plain except for two small brass hinges and the small latch on the front, also in brass. Saul carefully opened it, being so intent on his task he did not notice Johnny's smile warp his visage to something elemental.

Small diamonds glittered in reflected sunlight, mesmerising Johnny. For some reason he recalled his fascination of the bio-luminescence in the sea, that still sat with him.

"Not being an expert in these things, I'd say wow, they look beautiful to me. What are they?"

Saul had warmed to Johnny, possibly also bedazzled by the gems. "These, my friend, are all top rated stones. Their colour is graded 'D' – top grade, described in the trade as colourless, Johnny. There are no blemishes and we're looking at two carats each gem." He sighed, "Ah, you will not get any clearer then these."

Johnny hadn't taken his eyes from the diamonds, but he'd heard enough, "Right. Where to now, Saul? Club?"

"No, no, I want to see my wife Johnny. Please take me home to her," Saul said wistfully.

But Johnny still had business on his mind. "What about the stones Saul? What do you want to do about them? I mean where do you want to put them?"

Saul looked Johnny in the eye and stiffly affirmed, "They stay with me Johnny. They stay with me. Everything I have is at stake with these."

By the time the two had reached Saul's villa, he had relaxed a little and told Johnny something of his trip. "Not much to tell," thought Johnny, "Just a list of dinners, lunches and breakfasts with friends and family. Boring. Tel Aviv sounded like a shit hole."

He was standing just inside the front door looking into the open-planned living and dining room when a woman in a nurse's uniform appeared from the corridor leading to the bedrooms. She was pushing Maisie in a wheelchair. Johnny was actually shocked when he saw her. It was only weeks since the last time, but now she looked wretched. Her eyes were vacant and sunken, her once beaming face looked pinched and her fingers were gripping the arms of the chair like talons.

Saul had dropped his bag when he saw her and ran over to hug her and kiss her tenderly on the lips.

"She has been very good at times Saul, asking to use the toilet, even. She missed you didn't you Maisie?" said the nurse.

"What is wrong with her?" asked Johnny bluntly. Saul ignored Johnny and pulled the blanket up to her waist and tucked in more tightly around the edges. The nurse glanced at Saul, then at Johnny and said, "Maisie has Alzheimer's. Sometimes she can hardly recognize Saul let alone anyone else."

"Oh," said Johnny. He decided to go. "Okay I have to go, I have some business to do.

Look after them Saul. Make sure they are safe."

Saul knew Johnny wasn't talking about the nurse and Maisie. He looked at Johnny with contempt. Johnny didn't notice, he had an appointment to keep.

Half an hour later Johnny pulled into the Plaza de las Flores. He parked up and walked over the to the centre of the square and stood beside the stone fountain, shaped like a champagne glass. The camellias red blossoms were blood red in the circular bed around the fountain. He stood on the side of the square away from the parasol covered cafe tables scattered up to the fountain's west side.

Within a few minutes he was joined by an overweight Spanish man. He wore a jacket over his crumpled white shirt. He stretched out his hand, to Johnny. "Señor Fay, my uncle said you have a business proposition." As he put his hands on his hips, Johnny caught sight his gun holstered on his belt.

This was the Slug's nephew. He might be old now, but the Slug had risen through the ranks and had proved a useful contact for Johnny over the years. This time though the deal would require a more "hands-on" approach by the Old Bill and the Slug had recommended dealing with his nephew who was now a senior officer in the Guardia Civil.

"I suppose you've been informed of the job?" asked Johnny. "Look, all I am asking is how much?"

"Johnny, my uncle has already told you how much. It's three hundred thousand Euros and this is good price for what I do, yes?"

"Let's just be clear about this, when the job is done, I do not want you creeping back into me for someone else needing money. Is that clear? That's the finished price," replied Johnny stonily.

"Hey, you've long been doing business with my uncle. This is not going to happen

Johnny. I tell you three hundred thousand Euros. It is three hundred thousand Euros. No more. You have my word. Final price."

Johnny looked at the policeman and smiled. Johnny had his word. Yeah right. "I'll be in contact," he said and walked off towards his car.

Chapter Twenty-Five

Reunion – Part 1

Toni had a pleasant flight from Spain. She always travelled Business Class – for short haul even she wouldn't justify First Class. No, Business Class was quite attractive enough, she could recline her long legs in the better seats, sip a decent wine and even take a chance on the food.

Still, no matter where she went in the world, Toni always loved her grandfather's house. She remembered all the holidays when all of grandfather's sons and daughters came home with their families. There were great uncles, cousins, second cousins – everyone eating and drinking, walking in the hillside grounds and swimming in the pool that looked out across the Bay of Naples.

Grandfather always had many friends visiting, some she had known since she was a child. She was always treated like a princess by them, but she preferred to act the tomboy, climbing trees, fighting with her cousins and shooting clay pigeons from the cliff top. She always seemed to have memories of bright sunshine and laughter. Even Christmas was blessed by weak winter sunlight that managed to sparkle the decorations on the huge Christmas tree that sat by the tall patio double doors.

It was good to be back, having a good glass of sparkling Pinot Grigio from Trentino with her uncle.

She was only in the villa ten minutes, her bags had been taken to her room by one of the three maids, but she knew someone would be out on the marble terrace watching the sparkling sea, looking out to the Sorrentine Peninsula to the south and the looming, daunting shape of Vesuvius to the east.

"Ah my darling Toni, so good to see you. Your grandfather will be out in a minute, he's in the study," greeted her uncle. They spent a few minutes chatting about family things, a couple of upcoming dinners and then business.

Toni was unaware of the minor commotion inside the house. In spite of the controversial nature of many of the discussions held within the house, raised voices, bad manners and fuss would not be countenanced. Like any situation it was all most discretely handled, of course, within the villa.

The maid had gone into Toni's bedroom to perform her expected duties. There were Signorina Antonia's dresses and suits to be hung. Her washing had to be taken downstairs. The shoes had to be put away. The suitcases stored.

Natalie had worked for the Family for eight years and she knew her place. She knew discretion was a byword but her first responsibility was always to the 'capo in teste'. The Old Man was strict but fair. That all went through her mind when she found the package.

Natalie went through Toni's trousers, those that were balled up and chucked in the suitcase. In one of the pockets she found a packet, it was embossed. Natalie was polite, knew good etiquette but she was also from Naples. She also worked for the Family. The taste of this package spelt trouble. She left the unpacking and made her way to the study to see the Old Man.

Five minutes later the Capo made his way from the study to hallway leading to the terrace. He paused for a few minutes, sitting in his wheelchair in the wide marbled hallway looking through the huge patio doors at Toni and his son. They were sitting on the terrace laughing and sipping white wine. He sighed deeply. This was always bad business, he thought.

He manoeuvred his chair out onto the terrace and joined his family at the table. Toni leapt up and kissed him on both cheeks, saying how much she had missed him. He said nothing.

"What's the matter grandfather?" Toni asked plaintively. The Old Man ignored her but looked directly at his son. "Enough of the bullshit you two. Carlos, why don't you ask her why she is taking this shit?"

He flung the package Natalie had found onto the table in front of Carlos. It skittered across its metal top and Toni put her hand on it to stop it flying off. "She's even bringing it through customs, in her own luggage. It's trouble," he snarled.

It was Carlos's turn to look angry. He picked the package up, sucked the end of his finger and rubbed some of the packet's residue onto it, then tasted it. "What is this Toni? You bring shame to our family, using this stuff is trouble and bringing it in through customs is madness," Carlos said sternly.

Toni had been temporarily surprised by the discovery and the allegations. While she loved her uncle and her grandfather, no one was going to accuse her of something she hadn't done. "Now wait a minute. This is not mine, I found this in the man's belongings. He nearly caught me searching his apartment, so I never had time to put it back. That is why I'm there in Estepona, isn't it?" she argued, her dark eyes flaring.

Carlos paused. He looked at the package again, turned it over in his hands and then smoothed part of it out so he could look closer at the logo. Carlos looked at Toni more closely for a moment, "So you found this in his apartment?"

"Yes. I'd forgot all about that. I went through all of his belongings and I was looking at some of his paperwork and other things when this dropped to the floor and I picked it up and put in my pocket. Why? What's the issue?"

Carlos turned to the Old man and laid the smoothed out packet in front of him and then tapped the logo. It was a red embossed Rubber Duck. "Well up until now we had nothing to connect him to coke or Dutch Benny," said Carlos.

The Old Man waited before he said something. "Okay Carlos but this does not tell us anything, only that he has some of our product. It could have been sold to him, but it does not tell us by who. This is what we need to know. Where did it originally come from?"

Carlos sat straighter in his chair. "Capo, I have asked before, but why don't you let me do it my way?"

The Old Man patted Carlos's hand. "Ah my boy but no, because I do not want the resort littered with bodies. It attracts too much attention without certainty." He turned back to Toni. "I'm sorry I made such a hasty assumption my dear. Tell me more about your days in Spain, Antonia. Who does this man mix with?" asked the Old Man.

Chapter Twenty-Six
Reunion – Part 2

I guess it was a few months since I'd seen Toni when she phoned me. It was good to hear from her, my breath of fresh air. She said she wanted to see me as she was back in Málaga on business but she didn't want to see Johnny. She didn't even want him to know she was in the country.

That was fine by me and she asked me did Johnny still go to Casares up in the mountains. Mostly, when he had gone I knew he'd gone to meet Juan and the 'Winners' but now he'd taken to doing business at Juan's Málaga offices or villa.

So here I was sitting on the roof terrace at Antiguo Bar Nuevo looking out to the Plaza Casares. I'd always been fascinated by this village and had often thought about buying something up here. It had all I needed plus some welcome breezes to the unrelenting sun. I first noticed Toni walk across the triangle past the water trough. I'd always admired that water trough. It was square and divided into four separate troughs. The central square of stone was carved, its Muslim influence pronounced by four stumped minarets at each corner and only mitigated by a cross topping a central dome.

But this time I was concentrating on Toni. She didn't walk, she floated, the long white dress hugged her perfect figure. Her long black hair swung and bounced like one of those shampoo adverts.

I continued to look out to the square when I lost sight of her. I felt a little nervous and was swivelling my frosted glass of beer with one hand and rubbing my forefinger along the still fresh Two inch scar along my cheek. I caught myself doing it absent-mindedly. Anyway Toni was going to cheer up my miserable life for a few hours.

Then I noticed a slim shadow on the table I front of me. I got up and smiled broadly and gave her solid hug. "Hello Toni love. How have you been?" I motioned to the chair and pulled it out for her. She swept her legs across it and sat. I settled opposite her. It was then she noticed my scar. She didn't say anything for minute but put her hand up and touched it softly. I could swear her eyes misted over.

"Who do this to you Bill? Tell me?" I had never heard her lose her English grammar so badly before.

"No one. It's nothing, honest, Toni." I was touched by her tenderness. But she knew. Part of her amazing personality was her understanding and innate insight.

"That bastard. Why you still work with him Bill? He's no good for you. We've talked together too much for me not to know."

"He's alright, Toni. Really," I said half-heartedly.

I couldn't believe that she continued to speak in broken English. She was furious. "He treat you like shit. Me, like shit. He very selfish man. Now he do this to you. Stronzo!"

She couldn't stop. "Why you think I go? I will not be treated like that by nobody. He a very bad man. What happened?"

"We disagreed about Saul. And you're right. But forget him. How are you? I haven't seen you in weeks. What have you been up to?" There was no point in going into detail with Toni, she probably wouldn't understand.

Suddenly she leaned over and kissed me on the cheek and whispered, "Now you must trust me, Bill. Just trust me sweetheart." I didn't understand.

Then there was another shadow over the table. I hadn't seen him for years. He still had dark hair. He must have dyed it. How many years? Fourteen? More? He still looked immaculate, good looking and manicured. Possibly a little more refined with age.

I took a breath, but Toni leapt up smiling, "Oh Bill this is Carlos, my uncle. Uncle this is Bill."

I stood up. "Yeah. We've already met," I said and shook his hand.

Carlos moved around to one of the vacant chairs. "Of course, I remember you. You were with Johnny Fay, your partner, when we met in Gibraltar. We never did find Saeed."

I didn't like this one little bit, now it dawned on me who Toni's Grandfather was. Bad. On top of that fucking Saeed's name after all this time. Oh no, I certainly wasn't putting my neck on the line for Johnny Fay. "Partner?

No. I think you have things a little confused. I'm not a partner, I do some work for the man nothing else," I said quickly. Distance.

Carlos sat and stared at me while Toni said something in machine gun Italian. He glanced at her then looked back at me, "Is that scar part of your payment from Mr Fay?" He paused. "I must go, but I will leave the two of you to chat further."

He briskly got up from the table, kissed Toni on both cheeks and held out his hand to me. I shook it. "It has been a pleasure, Bill. I'm sure we'll meet again... Oh here, if you want to contact me, or call through Toni," Carlos said offering me his business card. I took it. "That's in case you have anything of interest for us to look at or tell me, you know." I looked at him, puzzled.

Then he leaned forward and produced a little piece of plastic from his jacket pocket. On it was an embossed Red Rubber duck logo. Oh fuck, fuck, fuck, fuck. Now Dutch Benny.

"Yeah, I'm sure we'll meet again," I replied taking the card and pretending to ignore the duck logo.

He headed for the stairs and disappeared.

That's when Toni told me about her family. About the villa above the Bay of Naples, about her grandfather and her uncle, about their long memories. Carlos and her grandfather had decided to send Toni over to keep an eye on Johnny. At the same time Carlos hadn't taken any chances and had a few gentlemen keeping an eye on Toni.

It seemed her grandfather liked Dutch Benny. He also regarded Johnny as a "shrewd" and "dangerous" man and Toni was there to figure out where Johnny's money came from. My face started throbbing again.

I said nothing to Toni that I shouldn't have. I admitted nothing.

But Toni knew me better than I knew myself. We found it easy to spend time with each other and while we now knew we were both skilled at putting people at ease, with us it was mutually natural. As I was planning my departure back to Estepona, Toni looked at me pleadingly. She reached over and gently ran her finger along my scar.

"I've booked a room in a cute hotel around the corner, Bill. Please come back with me," purred Toni. "I'd like for us to spend more time together." I felt my face flush. I hadn't expected this, surely. I was "Uncle Bill"? I looked at her big brown eyes and felt myself being pulled towards her.

"Is that to be my reward for stitching up Johnny Fay?" I asked.

"No Bill. You should know better, it's my reward, my heart," she promised.

The walk back to her hotel was something of a blur. The heady mountain air smelt as fresh as Toni, while we walked arms around each other's waist. It was close to the bar, but I still can't remember the route down and through the small cobbled streets which were more like alleyways.

Suddenly we were at a discrete door that lead into a terraced courtyard with potted palms and trees scattered around. It was a hotel I never even knew existed in the town. Beautifully hidden, distinct staff, traditional Moorish architecture. Toni dragged me laughing to the bar where she lined up five Tequila shots for each of us.

We sat at the bar and chatted animatedly. She asked about my ex-wife, a story of many decades ago. She listened intently, prodded me delicately. Then she told me when she first knew what the family business really was. We just talked and squeezed down the shots.

Then Toni grabbed my hand and pulled me towards the staircase.

Her room was beautiful. A large four-poster bed dominated the tastefully decorated room, sofa, a regal chest of drawers, walk-in wardrobe, marble bathroom with a free-standing roll-top bath.

Toni turned, swung the bedroom door to close and put her arms around my neck and kissed me passionately on the mouth, her tongue flicking past my lips. There was no talking. Toni was in control. She rubbed her body against mine.

Then as quickly as she had started she stopped. She walked over to a table a took a chilled bottle of champagne from an ice bucket. She poured two glasses, picked one up and walked towards the double doors to the large balcony. She beckoned me to follow.

As I walked closer, the view through the double doors was magnificent. The darkness of the evening was lit up by millions of stars and framed in front of it was Toni leaning over the stone balustrade, the bottom of her dress shimmering from side to side with the gentle evening air from the sea. I walked over to her and saw an uninterrupted view south to the sea, it shimmering in starry sympathy. The balcony was on its own, nowhere to overlook it, just views above red tiled roofs at awkward angles, past scrub-covered rocky mountain outcrops and out to sea.

"I love this place," whispered Toni, as I stood directly behind her. She reached behind her and grasped my groin gently but firmly. She placed her glass of champagne on the capstone beside her. Her other hand reached behind her and both unzipped my trousers.

She pulled and then she reached around her dress and pulled it above her hips. She leaned further over the balustrade and with the other hand enticed me closer to her, "Bill, I make my own choices and please, I want it now…" she screamed hoarsely.

Now I'm too much of a gentleman to go further. Needless to say. Toni and I stayed for a few more days in Casares. We talked of many things. She promised I would be all right and I should come with her to Italy. I trusted her but still said nothing that I shouldn't have. I still admitted nothing.

Never say never.

Chapter Twenty-Seven
Saul's Business

Saul was nervous. He was on his way to Juan's office. It was Friday, the beginning of one of the biggest weekends of his life. Maisie had another bad night but the nurse had been there to help and by the end of this weekend he should be all set up to meet in Juan's office to sort out the deal that could make sure he could look after his wife. He ignored the scenery, all he could think about was his wife and the diamond deal. But after all those years being 'Honest Solly', it stuck in his craw that he was reduced to a VAT fraud.

His mobile phone went off. He hit the hands-free button and answered, "Hello."

"Saul? Saul? Is that you? This is Jason, Jason Richards."

"Oh hello Jason, Saul here. I'm just on my way to the lawyers office."

"Listen Saul, me and you could do this deal on our own. It's costing me money from my side for Johnny but my understanding is you are the owner of the stones. Correct?"

Saul didn't like this. "But I think Johnny made the introduction, yes?"

"C'mon on Saul. Is he getting paid from your end too?" asked Jason.

"Well yes, but as I said he made the introduction." Saul could hear a sigh from the other end of the line.

"Well. All right if you are concerned about Johnny's cut, don't worry about it. We'll carry on as planned. I'll see you at the lawyers." And with that Jason hung up.

Saul was getting fed up with Johnny and was beginning to see that he wasn't quite the best friend he made himself out to be. Still he had set the deal up and he could do without upsetting him. He had too much on his mind without any further complications.

It was then the phone rang again. He could see it was Johnny's number.

"Hello Jon. What is it? I'm on my way to Juan's now," he said.

"Listen Saul I ain't too sure about this Jason. The guy I introduced you to. There's just something about him, doesn't smell right. So leave me out of this deal, alright, Saul?"

"Jon, I don't understand. Why? Is It the money? I will be paid Johnny, won't I? Or I will give back the merchandise to…" He could feel a rising sense of panic, he could hear his heart beating in his chest.

Johnny interrupted Saul. "Calm down. No, it's not the money Saul. That will be paid. It's who Jason is associated with, the people he represents. Look without being too blunt, I won't work with them for my own reasons if you know what I mean. It's not the deal, it's me Saul. You'll be fine besides Juan's looking out for you."

Saul's heart had stopped thumping so loudly but he still felt breathless. "Are you sure Johnny? Because I can cancel the meeting at the lawyers."

"Now look, don't be silly Saul. It's my personal reason. Think about the little woman at home. This deal gets you the help you both need. Go get it. Maybe we can do another deal another time," cajoled Johnny.

"Okay Johnny, I'll speak with you later," said Saul. After he'd hung up he looked at himself in the car mirror. He could see the corner of his eyes wrinkle as he smiled to himself. The full two hundred thousand. That would help Maisie.

He was still thinking of Maisie as he entered Juan's office. The receptionist opened the oak door and there sat Juan facing him, with Jason sitting opposite. He glanced around the office and 'expensive' was the word that came to mind. Unlike Juan's bare and glass-filled conference room, his office was more traditional. One wall was covered with books, mostly legal journals. His desk was solid oak with drawer legs and a green leather top. His desk chair was a wing topped leather chair and behind him were full length windows leading onto a small balcony. The other wall was covered with some family photographs but more commonly him with various celebrities and politicians along with legal certificates.

As Saul set his briefcase down by a chair he leaned

forward and shook hands with Juan, then Jason and they all exchanged the expected pleasantries. He sat facing Juan, next to Jason.

"Johnny not here with you then Saul?" asked Juan.

"No. This deal Is just with me," answered Saul.

"Oh, okay. Firstly, I have done the relevant paperwork, which you have both received by post or by hand, correct?" asked Juan again. The others nodded in agreement. Then he turned to Saul. "Saul would it be possible for the buyer to see exactly what he is buying?"

Saul's breathing was deeper than it had been when he entered first. He leaned down, picked up the briefcase up and placed it on the desktop. He reached in and took out the same wooden box he'd shown Johnny at the airport. The dark wood remained highly polished. Saul popped the small brass latch on the front.

The sparkle nearly lit up the room. Maintaining his professional composure Juan asked Jason. "Would you like to check your purchase?"

Playing the business game Jason replied, "Thank you. If you don't mind." He stood up and took out a pair of tweezers from his inside jacket pocket. From his other inside pocket he took out his jeweller's eyeglass. He looked into the box and peered more closely at the diamonds. Temporarily he forgot what he was doing and just stared. Then he gingerly picked up one of the stones with the tweezers and peered at it through the lens.

He repeated the process several times, then put down the tweezers and eyepiece. "I must congratulate you, Saul. They're just as described, unblemished two carats 'D' grade. No imperfections at all. I am very happy with them," Jason whispered.

He then picked up the eyepiece and put it into his inside pocket and pulled out a high-quality bonded envelope. He placed it in front of Saul, triumphantly.

Saul noticed Jason's smile but was staring blankly at the envelope. "What is this, Jason?"

"It's a banker's draft for the agreed amount of one point two million pounds."

"But I was expecting cash. Johnny mentioned cash," said Saul starting to worry again.

"Now hang on Saul, I never mentioned cash at any point. I'd never contemplate carrying that amount of currency on my person," said Jason sincerely. "It also weighs a hell of a lot."

Saul looked at Juan. Juan's mellifluous voice reassured an increasingly panicking old man. "No one mentioned cash Saul. Deals of this magnitude are mostly always paid with banker's drafts or wired. It's the way business is done over here my friend. I mean you didn't generally get suitcases full of cash in Hatton garden did you?"

"No, no, I suppose not," he replied but by this time he was hugging the wooden box, its clasp clipped shut.

"Look I'm sorry there's been some misunderstanding Saul. So here's what I propose. I have no problem with leaving the diamonds with Saul until the funds are cleared into the bank," offered Jason.

Saul looked at Jason and then across at Juan. He was breathing easier now. "What could go wrong?" he thought. The money would be in his account before he had to hand over the diamonds.

Juan struck. "Well I think it's only fair gentlemen, that the diamonds remain here in my safe until such time as the funds are cleared."

Saul looked at the box and then placed it back on the desk, picking up the envelope. "Right we'll sign a few documents, place these in my office safe, give Saul a receipt and we'll take the draft directly to the bank, agreed?" continued Juan.

Jason and Saul both nodded. Business was all but completed.

Even into the Sunday Saul remained nervous. He was feeding Maisie at the table in the kitchen, gently spooning some soup into Maisie's mouth. When the phone rang, he put the spoon down and said, "Be back in a minute my darling."

Saul walked over to the kitchen top and picked up his mobile. Before he could say anything. A man's voice spoke. "Hello. Is this Mister Saul Epstein?"

"Yes? Who is this, please?"

"Ah good, Mister Epstein. I've been instructed

to inform you from Barton's Bank, that the funds you deposited on Friday have now cleared and all instructions have been followed. Our Málaga office opens at nine a.m. on Monday morning and you can access them then. Is there anything else I can help you with Mister Epstein?"

Saul felt a flush of excitement, a wave of relief. "That's great news, Thank you. young man. No, there is nothing else thank you… Oh. By the way. Has everyone else been informed?"

"Yes. I have also informed Jason Richardson and Juan Rodriguez. All parties have been informed, sir. If there's nothing else sir. I will say have a good day and Goodbye."

Saul put the phone down slowly and turned to Maisie. He sat back down and gently touched her cheek. He noticed a tear rolling down her cheek. "Now, now Maisie darling, you shouldn't cry. I've just had the best news and we won't have any problems making sure you are well looked after. We might even take a trip back to London and see some friends."

He got up again and kissed her tear. "We will be alright now my love… We will be fine, now must just finish a little business."

He returned to his mobile and dialled Juan's number. "I understand the bank has been in contact with you Juan?"

"Yes. I had a phone call. Listen you should come in to the office first thing on Monday morning to give the stones to Jason, as he has now paid for them. He's due to fly out at ten a.m. which means it'll have to be early. Look shall we make it nine a.m? When the office opens." said Juan.

Chapter Twenty-Eight
It Weren't Me, Guv!

Tom's Sunday evening wasn't going as well as Saul's. In fact it was rapidly becoming the worst time of his entire life.

And his weekend had started so well. For Tom the small boat marina he'd bought with Johnny was a God-send. To be honest he had been getting a bit fed up of the constant partying. It had been a lifestyle he had only imagined would be found in films – beautiful girls, great food, all-day drinking, swimming pools, boats, sunshine and beaches. But there was only so much champagne he could drink and he had begun to find the hot weather and bright sunlight was the worst environment to be awakening with a daily hangover.

Running the marina gave him a little focus and it was a great environment for enjoying boats, sea and sun. He also didn't feel like such a sponging tit when he did a day's work. His ex-wife had always told him he was too caring, too socially responsible being an ambulance driver, he had figured it was only a matter of time before his soul caught up with him.

He was hoping to finalise a deal on the boat marina with Johnny and buy out his half. It'd be a good little earner, over time. He momentarily felt guilty about the fact it was Johnny who'd spotted the potential. Never mind Johnny always seemed to have his fingers in some pie or another.

Saturday morning wasn't exactly stressful. He had spent a few hours with an electrician Johnny had recommended. There was a problem with a couple of the mooring power points and the electrician had been in out to his van in the car park for various bits and pieces for a couple of hours. The marina jetties were busy with people preparing for the weekend, some fuelling up a day or two's sailing, others preparing to fuel themselves up with barbecues or parties on-board and without leaving the jetty.

"Well, Tom, that will have to do for now, until I can get some more parts in another two days, mate. Still all should be fine until Monday, except for berth 24, okay?" said Bob the electrician.

"Cheers, mate. When you want paying?"

"Well Monday when I have finished the job, would be nice, Tom."

"All right mate. See you Monday, Bob."

Tom headed back to his office, leaving Bob packing up his gear. He figured he only had another half hour here, finishing off some paperwork. He sat down in his big leather office chair and was shuffling through a sheaf of paper when he mobile phone rang.

"Hello darling. Yeah. Yeah. All right Tracy I will be back in a half an hour. Yeah. Milk, gotcha," he said.

After he had finished his work, he looked the office and went to his car. He enjoyed his black Mercedes 500.

It was like his boat – he couldn't believe how much he enjoyed using his relatively new toys. Milk, milk, milk, mustn't forget the milk. He also wanted to get some more fresh coffee too.

His mind didn't think of much as he drove along the beach road west into Estepona, he looked at the sparkling sea and the glamorous couples strolling along the esplanade looking for somewhere to have lunch. The sun was warm on his face.

He came to the end of Avenue Juan Carlos 1, to the small roundabout with the decorative fountain and turned right. Avenue Juan Carlos 1, was a wide road with shops and apartments down one side and close to the Carrefour, a car park. Considering it was the main north/south drag in Estepona, he always wondered why there always seemed to be so little traffic. He headed to the Carrefour Market up the wide boulevard with a central reservation of palm trees and tough leafed bushes and grasses. He drove along the dual-laned road for about half a mile and then turned left at a crossroads and came back on himself. Only 100 feet further on he swung nose-first into the pavement directly in front of the store. Happy days, he thought.

He looked up at the small Carrefour sign, nearly lost in the overwhelming salmon pink front of the five-storey building. He didn't especially like the supermarkets in Spain, they always felt cheap, a lack of pride in their displays compared to back home. They had some tasty grub, though.

He was only in there four minutes and wandered back out into the street, temporarily blinded by the strong sun. He headed for his car on autopilot. He had already taken his keys from his pocket and was fumbling for the sonic button before he noticed the police.

There were two police cars pulled up behind him, blocking him and the inside lane. There was another pulled into the space next to him. Two Guardia Civil were standing at the back of the Mercedes with their arms folded. Another two men were standing next to the car.

He'd recognised the police immediately, their mossy green shirts with bluey-green epaulettes, the same colour as their trousers – trousers tucked into the calf-high black boots that reminded Tom too much of the 'jack-boot' phrase. Worst of all he hated the hats that some wore. Those nasty rigid teresiana caps, stubby with peaks so short you wondered why they'd bothered. There was a military association with them and naturally being Europe they all had guns. But they never gave the impression they were carrying a lethal weapon. Half the time they were tucked in under an overlap of belly, or dangling just out of reach behind their right buttock.

But Tom didn't like guns. He remembered the few times he'd been called to a shooting incident. Most of the time you had to stop around the corner, have a conflab with the commander of the SO19 unit, then they'd dress you up in what looking like a bomb disposal suit. It wasn't quite as bad as that but by the time you had a helmet on, the body plates inserted into the Kevlar coat, you couldn't change gear or move the steering wheel. It was like being a bullet-proof and less colourful Mr Blobby. But he still hated guns.

"Er can I help you officer?" he asked nervously, addressing his question to the man closest and with the fanciest epaulettes. He could see people in passing cars looking at him curiously.

"Si señor, I believe you can. You can start by opening the trunk of your car, por favor," replied the Slug's nephew. He smiled.

Tom momentarily racked his brain to think if he'd left any weed in the car. No, there shouldn't be anything there. "Sure no problem. What is it you're looking for officer?"

Tom walked gingerly around to the back of the Mercedes and opened the boot. It was only then Tom noticed two further policemen behind him. They'd been on the other side of the supermarket exit, presumably to cut him off he made a break for it. He looked at the officer in the eye, but the policeman was staring into the car boot.

He turned back to Tom, he unbuttoned his holster and drew out his Star model BM 9mm parabellum.

"Get down on the ground. Down on the floor now!" he screamed, there seemed to be a cacophony of shouts from every angle, some in Spanish, some nearly in English. Worst of all there was the cocking of the guns. Click, click, click.

The next few seconds were a daze, but his chest felt like it had been hit by an England prop forward. His back didn't feel much better. His hands were roughly cuffed and he was hauled to his feet to stare over the lip of the of the boot. It was empty and clean apart from a small clear plastic box in which he kept tools and such like. It was empty except for the plastic box and… a clear white package and a US army issue 45 calibre Browning pistol.

His head was still swimming. He looked again. What was in the package? Shit it looked like coke. "That is not mine. I swear to God it's not mine. You have to believe me. It's not mine," he sobbed.

"Of course not amigo. You can tell that to the judge, but for now, you are going to be charged for drug dealing, I would say, and certainly possessing an illegal firearm," said the Slug's nephew gleefully.

Tom was thinking. Was he dreaming? Had he been spiked and was having a dose of the paranoias? Shit. What would Johnny do? "Listen I am innocent. I don't know how it got there, but it was not me… …listen if it's about money…"

A look of self-righteousness furrowed the policeman's brow. "Señor, you are already in serious trouble. Do not add bribery to your problems."

Tom shut up. He thought later he must have gone into shock because he couldn't recall anything until he came out of a daze, hands cuffed behind his back sitting at a desk. He was in a glass-walled office in the corner of a busy patrol room. The door was open. The noise – people shouting abuse, questions repeated again and again, crying, the hum of computers, the ringing of phones and soft subsonic moan of over-worked air-conditioning units, was unbearable.

That was the sound. The smell was worse. He could detect the faint odour of urine, a lot of heavy body odour and some over-powering aftershave. The office looked new yet it had high ceilings narrow, tall windows with bars across them, very much in a traditional style.

"Please get in touch with Johnny Fay, my business partner," pleaded Tom.

"This is not a business issue. I think you need a lawyer, my friend not your partner," warned the policeman.

When Saul was getting news of the completed money transaction, Tom was sitting in front of John Jenkins from the British Consul. Tom had had a lousy night's sleep. The bed was uncomfortable, it was cold and there were people snoring, farting, screaming and crying all night. Every time a policeman came near him they smiled like they knew something he didn't and refused to listen to anything he had to say. He'd been quizzed and questioned for hours. None of it made sense.

John Jenkins wasn't much better. Mr Jenkins was a full-time foreign office man seconded to the Málaga area consulate. It was one of the busiest British Consulates in the world simply because of the number of Brits who insisted on coming there on holiday and getting pissed and fighting or exposing themselves or falling from balconies or not paying bills or insulting the locals or smoking weed. Frankly, thought Jenkins, they were generally a complete shower and deserved everything they got. For some reason most of his charges seemed to think that by screaming "I'm a British national" loud enough, the Spanish authorities would simply let them go. Morons.

This one was a bit different. It wasn't as if he hadn't handled drugs and guns before on the Costa del Crime but it wasn't your average day. Half a kilo of coke and a handgun.

"Look I tell you I have never seen these things in my life. Why would I lie?" said Tom.

"Not to put too fine a point on it, you'd lie because if you admitted it, you'd be automatically banged up," replied Jenkins. "Look, I can only help you if you give me something, like who would want to do this to you and what reason would they have. Anyone?"

"I don't know. None. No reason. But someone has done this to me."

"Look here Mister Papworth, you were found with half a kilo of cocaine and a hand gun in a car which is registered to you, that you were driving at the time. They have a clear case. You're looking at serious time here. Depending on the presiding judge and the prosecutor it could be 15 years. That's the bad scenario. Another thing, officially here there's no plea bargain, but sometimes they offer it handing down a reduced sentence if there's co-operation. Be aware, it can help," Jenkins advised.

Tom put his head in his hands and began sobbing. Fifteen years… fifteen years.

Jenkins got up from his metal chair. This part always made him feel uncomfortable. The crying, the realisation that their life as they knew it was over. "Goodbye Mister Hepworth. I'll be in contact."

As Jenkins left, the Slug's nephew appeared. For a moment, Tom glanced up and randomly thought, why do so many of these coppers have such tight and ill-fitting trousers.

Tom didn't think it for long. The policeman spoke softly, hissing like Kaa from Walt Disney's Jungle Book, "Listen my friend. I may be able to help you in some small way. You sign this paper and you are given two and a half years for the charges. You plead guilty, yes?"

For the time since he could remember, Tom looked at a man with utter contempt. He looked up and saw Jenkins still standing in the doorway. Jenkins' look said "Take it" and he turned and left. Tom's hope disappeared with that quick look. His contempt dissipated and a feeling of abject defeat filled his soul. He slumped in his chair. His head dropped.

He fumbled in front of him without looking and picked up the pen.

Saul had been barely able to sleep. He knew he had to be at Juan's office for eight a.m. The deal would be finished and he and Maisie would be okay. It went over in his head time and time again.

He felt elated but weary when he joined Jason and Juan at the lawyer's office. Saul sat next to Jason and both across from Juan. Same as last time. Juan had already taken the small dark wooden box from his safe. He slid it over to Saul, who opened the box, verified the contents and then shut it. He hesitated for a second then slid it on to Jason.

When it reached Jason, he immediately lifted the clasp and looked into it. His eyes widened as he opened as the lid. Saul could see the look in Jason's eyes, the look he'd seen on so many before. They saw the value, the wealth, the power of the diamond. They didn't see what Saul saw, the workmanship of the cut, the colour, the shape, the wonder of nature's beauty.

Jason's hands were shaking as he closed the lid and shut the clasp. "It has been a pleasure doing business with you Saul, and you Juan. Sorry about Johnny missing out. Perhaps we'll meet again," he said. He got up to leave.

"The pleasure is all mine Jason," replied Saul.

"Well, I take it we are all happy at the outcome?" Juan asked them both. They nodded affirmation.

Then Jason said, "Well I have to rush as I'm catching a flight in forty-five minutes." They all shook hands.

Saul lingered with Juan as Jason left. "Well thanks

Son of Lucifer

Juan. I'm going down to the bank, after some breakfast. It opens at ten a.m. Adios." He left and felt there was now a little spring in his step.

Saul was waiting outside Barton's Bank when staff drew the blinds and opened the glass double doors. It might have had a wealth management arm but the branch looked like it should have been in Bethnal Green – a corner site in a typical apartment-cum-shop building, looking towards the Avenuye Palama de Mallorca and a pedestrian precinct. But it was Barton's, that well-known British high street institution, nonetheless.

The teller had a steaming cup of coffee next to her and a look of "Not already" on her face as she took Saul's banking card. "Can you give me a balance on my account please?" Saul asked, looking up into her face. She ran the card's magnetic strip through a scanner attached to her computer and checked the numbers off. Saul entered his pin number.

She glanced at the screen, picked up a bank slip and wrote a figure down and passed under the glass partition to Saul. She didn't mention the figure. It was the customer's private information. She waited.

Saul looked at the slip. He could feel an instantaneous sweat break out, his heart was pounding. There had to be some mistake. "I… I'm sorry miss but this says the account only has eleven thousand four hundred Euros. There has to be a mistake!"

The teller looked back at the screen. And then at Saul. He looked grey. "No Señor. There is no mistake."

Suddenly Saul found Oliver, his banker, next to him. "Saul, Saul, I was just about to call you. I've had head office on the phone, they have just told me that draft you presented us with was stopped by our fraud department."

Saul said nothing. He looked at Oliver, his face white, his mouth opening and closing but not a sound coming out. He then turned on his heels and ran out of the bank, leaving Oliver and most of the bank staff watching him.

Juan was taking a phone call when Saul burst into his office, the receptionist hanging behind looking frantic at the sight of a mad man. Saul ignored the phone in Juan's hand.

"The diamonds... The diamonds. Where are the diamonds Juan? Where are the gems? Where's Jason?"

"Calm down Saul, you know where they are. What's going on?" He whispered something into the phone and hung up.

"He's stolen the diamonds. He has swindled the diamonds from me with a fraudulent banker's draft. There's no money," Saul sobbed.

"Sit down and calm down. If that's the case then we should phone for the police, they should be able to get him at the airport. Let me call them," reassured Juan. But as he reached for the phone handset again and began to dial, he paused and looked Saul directly in the eyes.

"Saul. The V.A.T. You have paid the V.A.T. on those diamonds? If you haven't you could be looking at two to five years in prison if we report this. Saul?"

Saul said nothing but leaned over to the phone and disconnected the line. He looked at Juan with tears in his. "My God Saul. What were you thinking, man?"

Saul only whispered. "I'm finished. My life is over. My poor Maisie."

Chapter Twenty-Nine

Revelations

I'd had a great weekend in Gibraltar. Peace and quiet, away from Saul, from Tom but especially Johnny. I was getting too old for all this shit. It was beginning to get me. There was the fear element but it was something else too.

Unfortunately Monday brought it all into focus. I went around to Johnny's villa just before lunchtime. I'd decided to go over some supplier contracts with him and I just didn't fancy sitting in the club. We were sitting in the living room when the door was hammered furiously.

"Go get that Bill," Johnny ordered.

When I opened the door. I couldn't believe what I was looking at. It was Saul. He looked terrible, his eyes were red, his face ashen, his tie was askew and what hair he had looked as if he had been pulling it out. "Saul? What the fuck has happened? Come in, come in. Saul? Are you alright?"

I could barely hear him. "He has ruined me Bill."

"What? Who? Come in. Come in," I said. I then shouted for Johnny. But he was already behind me and took one of Saul's arms and led him down the steps and across to the settee in front of the fireplace.

"He has ruined me Jon."

"Who has Saul? Who has?" asked Johnny sympathetically.

"That bastard Jason. The banker's draft was a fraud. Oliver told me and this Jason person has walked away with the diamonds," Saul could barely speak.

I was surprised by Johnny's response. "I fucking knew it. I told you, didn't I? That's why I pulled out of it. I knew Jason was dodgy." I looked at him. Johnny wasn't looking at Saul, he was looking at me, flicking his head towards the doorway with a sneer on his face. He didn't have any more time for old Saul, this thirty seconds of sympathy or reassurance was already too much trouble.

I could feel my face flushing. Fucking Johnny-boy, no sympathy let alone tea, just get rid of him. I took Saul's arm. "Come on Saul, you're in no condition to drive, let me take you home," I said.

There was no resistance. After Johnny's outburst, everything seemed sucked out of Saul – energy, spirit, will, life, even a reflection in his eyes. I gently led him out of Johnny's villa to my car.

Saul was shaking in the passenger seat, barely capable of speaking, when I remembered I had left my car keys on the coffee table in the living room. Time slowed down for me after I opened the front door and entered the room.

Johnny was sitting on the same sofa that Saul had staggered to. But he didn't look like Saul, there was no worry, despair, pain… no Johnny's face screamed greed, triumph, power. Unassailable power.

On his lap was a dark polished wooden box. It's lid was flipped open and the small brass latch hung down. Johnny was laughing, he was letting diamonds drip from his fingers into the box. He repeated it again and again, laughing ever harder.

I was mesmerised. He looked up and saw me. His laugh turned to a sneer. "See Bill. Remember? I'm always right, greed, play people's greed. That fucking Jew boy thought he'd cheat. Now look at him."

"No Johnny, it wasn't greed. It was desperation, it was love for his wife. But I'm the fucking idiot for thinking you'd understand that. For fuck sake Johnny what have you done?" I whispered.

"Boo fucking hoo. At trade cost these beauties are a million pounds. These are clean so they have to be worth up to one point five million pounds," revelled Johnny.

I had nothing else to say. I didn't know what to do. I rubbed my scar and picked up my keys and turned around to leave. Johnny didn't stop. "Yeah crawl off Bill. By the way, I made a bit more on that other mug Papworth. Drugs and guns. Who'da thought. Come up in the world ain't he? Now all I do is sell everything he owns. I'm still in my prime."

I felt sick. I hadn't heard anything about Tom. Mind you I had spent the weekend up in Gibraltar. I'd had to get away from Johnny.

All the way to Saul's home he just sat there in the passenger seat staring out the passenger window, his hands clasped in his lap. He hadn't even put his seat belt on. Any joviality had been sucked out of him. I kept glancing at him, as if I expected him to throw himself out the car door. I kept the radio off.

I simply didn't know what to say to him. I knew Saul was upset enough about simply being involved with something illegal. But this, this scam of Johnny's had ruined him. He'd been working hard for nearly sixty years and everything was gone. His wife was dying in one of the most soul-destroying ways.

I kept quiet as long as I could. "Look Saul, don't worry. We'll try to sort something out. I'll make a few calls and see if that gets us anywhere." I had to give him some reassurance.

Saul still said nothing, but I could see tears rolling down his cheek, his head now resting on the door window. Even when I pulled into Saul's drive he said nothing, he simply opened the car door and stumbled out. I got out my door and offered to go in with him but he ignored me.

I stood at the driver's door and lit a cigarette. I couldn't leave, not yet. It was another clear night, the stars oblivious to the pain below. I felt a little chilled. I was putting out the cigarette when I saw the nurse hurry out the front door two overnight bags in her arms. She paused and looked at me, and hurried out through the gate without saying a word.

Bollocks. Saul didn't want anyone around except Maisie. He was probably pouring his heart out to her even though she was now barely capable of watching the Teletubbies. Bollocks, I should go.

I guess I was almost at the club when I turned the car around. Something told me that should return and check on him, help him somehow.

I pulled back into the drive again and hurried to Saul's front door. It was ajar. Ajar. That gave me the creeps. In the old days in London that usually meant something bad. I pushed it open and stood in the doorway, waiting. The lights were all on.

Saul's hallway was a large one, more like an atrium. Directly across from the front door were steps down to the open living room which looked onto the darkened windows hiding the pool and patio area. To my left was a doorway to a kitchen and dining room. Behind the front door on the other side I knew was a door to a downstairs bathroom and the staircase to the mezzanine floor. Under the stair case was another door leading to a bedroom with en suite.

I could see all the way through to the living room and it looked like Maisie was asleep on the sofa in the living room. She wasn't moving and there was no noise in the house at all.

I remember the next second as if it was a year. I called out loudly, "Saul? Saul? Are you there? It's Bill." I swung the door right back and stepped into the hall. The cicadas outside were deafening. There was the faint lemony scent of some Evening Primrose and the acrid smell of bleach. Poor Maisie.

I noticed the shadow first. Saul's shadow suspended. Saul suspended. Saul was hanging from a rope from his metal balcony on the mezzanine floor into the atrium. There was a pool of liquid under him. Piss, I suppose.

I always think I took longer than I should have to get to Saul, that if I hadn't stood and looked and hesitated, he could have been saved.

"Oh no. Saul. For fuck's sake man. Not that," I spoke out loud. I remember he was too high for me to reach his legs to support him, let alone cut the rope around his neck. I ran up the stairs and looking down I could see that he hadn't hung himself, he'd thrown himself off and snapped his neck. From what I know he could have still been alive choking slowly for minutes before he actually died.

I managed to climb over the bannisters and reach far enough down to touch his neck. No pulse, even his body heat had begun to ebb.

That's when I thought of Maisie. I left Saul for the coppers to sort out and ran to the sofa in the living room. Her eyes were open and there was drool dripping from her bottom lip but there was no breathing. There were red flecks around her mouth. It was then I noticed the red cloth cushion lying on the floor next to her head.

Poor Saul. Poor Maisie.

I sat down on the floor, my back on the sofa seat and looking away from Maisie, took out my phone and called the police.

I don't know how long it was before the police and the ambulance turned up. I hadn't moved by the time the first coppers showed up. Then it got fun, the senior Guardia Civil turned up. I recognised him immediately. Adriano, the big Pooh-Bah. Nephew of the Slug. Just my luck, I didn't like or trust him any more than his fucking uncle. On the other hand. we had paid him a shit load.

I watched the two covered bodies of Saul and Maisie Epstein being pushed down the drive next to each other towards the private ambulance. Together, ironic. Adriano had been asking me questions for a while but being Johnny's associate, in a most polite, thoughtful and apologetic way. I was amazed his squidgy little fingers could grasp a pen to write in his notebook.

"Look I've got to go, this has been an exhausting experience. If there's anything else I can help you with, just let me know. You have my numbers," I said suddenly needing to escape the activity, the revolving lights, men shouting instructions, others whispering, tape being streamed.

"Thank you Señor Bill. You've been very helpful, as always. By the way did you hear about Señor Papworth?"

I hesitated. I'd forgotten what Johnny had said earlier about Tom, but nicked? "No… What's happened to him?"

"I'm afraid I had to arrest him Señor. It turns out he was a very bad man. I searched his car and we found drugs and arms. Your friends seem to be having very bad luck Mr Bill. Take care of yourself," said Adriano, squeezing my arm.

That's when something changed completely. A spell had been broken. A soul had been reclaimed. The question for me was whether the soul could be saved. I remember getting about five minutes down the road after I took my last look at Saul and Maisie in the back of the ambulance, when I pulled over.

Had I made a decision? Could I make the call? Should I destroy decades of friendship? Friendship? What friendship? I rubbed my scar again. Good times? I was tired of those good times. I wanted to fish, eat leisurely lunches, drink good wine, watch the football and rugby, peace and fucking quiet.

Time to make a phone call.

It was the next day when I drove slowly to Johnny's villa. There was some stuff I wanted out of the bungalow in the garden and from the living room, but I didn't much fancy chatting with Johnny. I drove slowly up his drive hoping he wouldn't hear the car. I suppose he didn't. He was obviously too engrossed in chatting with his Winners. When I got there. I recognised the cars of Oliver, Juan and Mark.

In some ways that was good for me since it would rein Johnny's temper in, at least a little. Besides since it was my gun I wanted from the bungalow, I wasn't too bothered. I was so angry with Johnny right now even I might shoot him.

I walked up under the arches across the lawn and behind the pool to the bungalow. I had expected they would be all sitting outside but they weren't. It didn't take me long to gather what I wanted into a holdall and walk back towards the villa, along the top of the pool and past the bell tower. I started to hear the murmur of voices as I approached the gallery entrance to the house. I didn't mount the steps into the gallery room but stood by them at the doorway to the living room.

Of course the first voice I heard was Johnny's. "I want everything sold Mark: the apartment, the yacht, the marina. Sort the paper work out quick as you can. Got it? And Oliver, the joint bank account with Tom's funds in it: transfer everything into mine and close his account today by end of business."

Then it was Juan. "You want me to hold on to the diamonds till you find a buyer?"

"Yeah but not at the office. Keep them at your home. I also want you to keep an eye on the sales with Mark so I stay within the law. The last thing I need is some silly mistake to fuck this up," Johnny replied.

I'd heard enough. Johnny was in his George Peppard mood of "I love it when a plan comes together". I walked up the steps into the gallery and then up into the living room. I went directly over to the bookcase and picked a few of my things up and took some of my paperwork from a desk drawer. I didn't say a word to any of them. I had the gun sitting at the top of the open holdall and just put the other things around it. My heart was racing, I could feel a bead of sweat forming on my nose. But I was going through with it.

They were sitting on two sofas facing each other over a mahogany coffee table, paperwork strewn across it. No doubt by this time tomorrow he'd be fleecing Saul's estate too.

Johnny said nothing when I first came in, but watched me as I gathered my gear. Then he barked, "Where you been Bill? Bill? Where do you think you're going? Bill. I'm talking to you."

The others said nothing. I looked at him once, just before I turned and walked out the front door. My mouth was set firm and I found myself rubbing my scar again. We locked eyes for a moment and then I left. It was the last time I saw Johnny Fay. Joe Wilkins. Lucifer.

But I could still hear him. "Fuck him. He'll be back, he needs me," he told the others.

Little did he know.

Facts were facts – it was over twenty years and Carlos was still looking out for who had done Benny. He wouldn't stop. Then there was Saeed's brother. No doubt Carlos would have used whatever information he could get to make deals, so he'd be looking too. Who else? Lenny, Bentley, Blondy, Papworth? And all the others.

I had a meeting to keep. Up in Casement Square in Gibraltar. There was low cloud over the Rock and it threatened rain. It was the same place where all those years ago I'd met Carlos for the first time. And there he was, same table, same restaurant – The Tunnel. It was busy in the square, tourists staring at maps, taking photographs, with locals meeting for coffees and doing business. I walked over to where Carlos was sitting on his own. He was staring at a family organising themselves for a holiday picture on a bench in front of an ornamental bush in a stone container and stirred his coffee absent-mindedly.

I suppose this meeting had its risks but I wasn't bothered about that. I had made a few decisions and this was simply the best way to get the ball rolling. I had my own plans, helped by Toni.

Couples and groups sat at the tables around him, but the coffee drinkers sitting on the table behind Carlos weren't there for enjoyment. Both still wore sunglasses even though the day was dull. The eyes may have been hidden but the sweeping heads showed they were most attentive to the square's activity. They both wore expensive hand-made black suits, silk ties and gleaming black shoes. I knew they were expensive suits, they were hand-cut not to show the gun bulge.

Carlos looked up as I got to within a few feet of his table. He stood up. I could see he was wearing his favoured off-white trousers, brown shoes, simple white shirt with a smart sports jacket. He stuck out his hand, shook mine, smiled a reassuring smile and then gestured me to sit down.

"Hello Bill. Toni tells me you want to speak with me

about some serious matters," he said. "Shall I order you something first?"

"Yes please, an espresso. It's been a long week, I need something to keep me ticking over. Well as you might have realised, Johnny Fay is a dangerous man. He's also known as Joe Wilkins and Lucifer," I said. I think this was the first time in decades I'd spoken all those names aloud to another person. It was like a magic spell. The incantation felt like it lifted a weight from my soul.

We had two more espressos by the time I had told Carlos all about Johnny. I told him what I knew of what happened to Dutch Benny. He told me about when he'd watched the police at Benny's home. I told him what Johnny had done with the coke. I told him what had happened with Saeed. I told him what happened to Saul, to Tom, to others, to me. I told him I wanted to retire and fish.

"Well Bill, I understand your position. You should take a holiday. Toni tells me she has invited you to Naples. No doubt my father will enjoy your company, especially some stories from London in the sixties. Now please excuse me I must call him with the news," said Carlos.

We shook hands again and the two Men in Black looked around the square. Before I had taken a step Carlos was already phoning the Old Man and I knew that within seconds he would untie Carlos's hands and what must be done, would be done.

Chapter Thirty
Apocalypse

Dr Graham had become more engrossed in my tale as the weeks went on. He spoke less and less, took fewer notes and became more intent on what I was saying. He sucked his pen ever-more vigorously, but I suspect he found the denouement something of a letdown.

I was in Italy with Toni and a few weeks later we were joined by Carlos. The Old Man seemed to like me and Carlos had been correct, he was always asking about London in the sixties and seventies and so I was invited over to the family villa again for a quick tale.

It seemed Adriano met his uncle to discuss business once a week. While the two saw each other frequently at family events, they'd decided that privacy was best for ongoing business, unless there was a crisis. This particular meeting was to be historic. It was to be their last. The Slug was retiring. His cut of the three hundred thousand Euros just iced the cake. Since the Slug was passing on to Adriano his book of notes, contacts, dirt and accounts they would stick to procedure.

They had long ago decided the car made the best place for the weekly meet. Adriano's weekly lift for his uncle screamed plausible deniability but gave plenty of time for mutual updates. The Spanish press initially blamed Euskadi Ta Askatasuna (ETA) for what had happened. Headlines speculated over the death of a local police legend on his retirement, others commented on the family tragedy uncle and nephew, but those only lasted a day or two. Then chosen editors received anonymously delivered documents about bribery and corruption and questions began to be asked about the two policemen.

Witnesses said the two had got into Antonio's private Mercedes and when he started the engine, there was a problem with the starter catching. Then there a flash and a fire followed by a ear-ringing bang. Nothing was left of the car but mangled metal, the street showered with shards of window glass. The bodies were never found. Part of the engine block was found a street away.

The news of their deaths overwhelmed the Spanish press and other mysterious incidents in the Costa del Sol at around the same time disappeared among endless lines of type. They lay as paragraph mentions buried within the papers' domestic news.

Oliver had been Johnny's banker for decades. Even if he didn't know where all the cash came from, he knew where it was. He was in his kitchen making coffee. When the police arrived the coffee machine was fully loaded and ready to go. So was Carlos's man. It was one shot to the temple.

Mark had been sleeping, when he'd heard a noise, so said the police. He was in his sleeping clothes, the bed sheets tossed and rumpled. He was found at his patio doors with a bullet in the forehead and one in the heart. It seems the intruder wasn't in the pool area but waiting in Mark's house until he came back in.

It was Carlos who told me about Jason. I had told him about Tricky Dickie and his part in Saul's downfall. He had the same heart as Johnny – black and hardened. That heart was broken when he answered the front door of his Madrid apartment and two bullets entered it.

Carlos had taken an interest in Saul's story. I later realised why. It would give him an opportunity to be reimbursed for Dutch Benny's coke. Juan wasn't as lucky as the others, except that his wife was away seeing family. His dispatch came with more "'persuasion", several broken fingers, cracked second and third ribs, popped kneecap and facial lacerations, according to the autopsy. The police had found his safe open and concluded one of his former clients had been disenchanted with Juan's defence skills. One bullet to the head, one to the heart.

No diamonds were found.

It was DI Elder who'd told me about Johnny. I took a call on my mobile a few days before Carlos returned to Italy.

"Bill, this is DI Elder. Where are you? I was getting worried."

"Well that's nice of you, if unexpected," I replied cautiously. "I'm on holiday in Italy, first one in a while, as far as I'm concerned. How're you and why you phoning?"

"Haven't you heard about Johnny Fay?"

"To be honest Mr Elder, I don't give a fuck about Johnny Fay. I left a couple of weeks ago and me and him are finished. He can do his own dirty work from now on," I said vehemently.

"I see. Can't say it surprises me except it took you so long. You timed it well, though," he said.

"Timed it well? What do you mean Mr Elder?"

"Some blonde bimbo found him dead yesterday morning," he paused for effect.

"Dead?" I said sounding surprised. "What do you mean dead? How?"

"She said he got up early in the morning, saying what a beautiful morning it was and he was going to admire the sunrise from the pool area."

"Yeah, Johnny liked the sunrise. He was always telling me to engorge myself on it, that it was beautiful. He was probably also thinking about his bank accounts," I replied sarcastically.

"She didn't hear anything except a splash. She assumed he was taking a dawn swim. But he had two bullets in his head and two in the heart," explained Mr Elder. "It sounds like she was pretty upset when she found the pool had turned red and Johnny was lying face down in it."

"My God. Who did it?" I asked, realising immediately what had happened and who had happened.

"Well we don't know. But Bill I did see a photo of what was found in the pool with him."

"In the pool, what do you mean?" I was unsure of where this was leading.

"It was a plastic package with a red embossed Rubber Duck logo. Does that ring any bells Bill?" asked Mr Elder, in a way that hinted he already knew the answer. "Well let me remind you Bill. That coke that Bentley and Blondy ended up with was all wrapped like that."

"I'll take your word for it, Mr Elder. It was a long time ago. I'm gutted to hear about Johnny but thanks for letting me know. Maybe I'll avoid the Costa del Sol for a few weeks. Nice to chat Mr Elder."

And so that was that. Johnny Fay, Joe Wilkins, Lucifer back burning in hell and there but for the grace of God I could have been with him.

Dr Graham sighed deeply when I told him the end of the story. "Is that it?" he asked. He wanted more. I looked at him. His eye's looked pleadingly, he leaned forward in his chair. He had been drawn into Johnny's world just by me speaking about it, the black magic woven by Lucifer.

As for any more of the story, who knows?

Chapter Thirty-One

Loose Ends

Walter McGowan swivelled on his chair and looked out the window. The floor to ceiling glass gave his office the privilege of overlooking the railway lines running into Waterloo, Vauxhall Station and the rather optimistically named Vauxhall Pleasure Gardens. He sighed. He'd always wanted an office on the other side of the building, looking at the Thames and up to the Palace of Westminster. Vauxhall housing estates just didn't have the same appeal.

Still, he thought, at least it's better than Century House. He'd hated that soulless piece of sixties architecture and was pleased when he'd moved in here in 1994. He'd always had difficulty describing the new building to people until he'd come across some article or another about the architect, Terry Farrell. His influences for the design were a cross between Battersea Power Station and Mayan and Aztec temples, apparently.

McGowan had an immaculate grey suit, starched white shirt and red silk tie. He was beginning to go bald on top, a bit early for a forty-year-old, he thought. He worked for MI6 and enjoyed his desk job with a smattering of overseas travel. Mostly he "liaised" and lunched in some of London's finest eateries purely for work, you understand.

The phone rang and McGowan put the receiver to his ear. His secretary told him that his conference call was ready and they were only waiting for the permanent secretaries from both the Home Office and Foreign Office to join the line. "McGowan," he announced.

DI young was already waiting and both were nearly immediately joined by the ministers. It was to be a brief conversation. He listened for a few moments, scribbling a note or two on his desk pad. "Thank you Mr Elder for the summary," said McGowan.

"Well, we'll find it hard to find another Joe Wilkins," said the man from the Foreign Office. There was a grunt of agreement from the man in the Home Office.

Then it was DI Elder's turn to comment, "What about Tom Papworth and the Epsteins?"

"What about them?" said the man from the Home Office. "The Home Secretary's view is that they're collateral damage, I am afraid. We can do nothing without exposing ourselves."

"And that is the view of the Foreign Secretary, these issues are not to be mentioned again. Clear?" said the man from the Foreign Office. In unison both permanent secretaries bade goodbye and hung up.

McGowan listened to Mr Elder. First of all there were profanities, then there was comment. "Yes I agree," said McGowan. "As you say in your business, a right jumped up little fuck. And I suppose thinking of Papworth and the Epsteins as collateral damage is distasteful but you know what else Wilkins was into.

Son of Lucifer

This falls under National Security, I'm afraid. We all have to keep quiet. Goodbye, I'll see you next month."

McGowan now turned to his computer, its Tempest-standard screen not reflecting the light coming through the windows. After entering his password, he entered search parameters and called up a file. A large file. A file that largely held scanned documentation. An old file.

McGowan printed a couple of pages, then logged out of his computer. He picked them up from his printer sitting on elegant ash bookshelving, moving as he did so for the frosted glass door in the green glass wall. He walked down the hall, thinking the same thing that he thought at least three times a day, "how come it's so quiet and unhurried for such a dangerous organisation?"

After a few moments he stopped outside an office marked "Accountant". He knocked, but walked straight in, past half a dozen men and women beavering away at their desks, faces illuminated by their computers.

"Ah, Mr Wolf, glad I caught you in," said McGowan, to a small, bald bespectacled man also dressed in a suit. "I have a Closure Notice for you, a D-45."

"Oh dear, oh dear. No one we know I hope?" said Mr Wolf sincerely.

"No, fortunately. However, it's an account that's been open for some time, a very long time," explained McGowan.

"I see, I see. Name, codename and number please."

McGowan handed over the few pages of A4 he had printed off. Mr Wolf turned to his computer and logged in. After a another series of security operations, including his fingerprint scanner, ID badge magnetic strip code and a sixteen digit hexadecimal password, Mr Wolf pulled up the appropriate file.

Mr Wolf whistled, which surprised McGowan. He'd never heard Mr Wolf whistle.

"My, my this has been a very active account. It's also one of the oldest we currently deal with at least in terms of being uninterrupted. See that reference number, that's the Cold War era," said Mr Wolf enthusiastically. He turned to look at McGowan. "I suppose it's going to be hard to replace him? I say Walter, the D-45, natural or…"

"With extreme prejudice, Francis, with extreme prejudice, but nothing to do with us. Chickens and roosting, chickens and roosting, Francis," said Walter.

"I see, I see. Alright I've started the thirty day process. We'll tie off loose ends, close accounts, do the usual. Well that's the Joe Wilkins, AKA Johnny Fay, file sorted out. Codename Lucifer terminated."

THE END

Tom Papworth returned to the UK after serving 30 months for drug and arms offences in a Spanish prison. To this day he is still fighting to clear his name from all charges.

Kenneth Noye is serving a life sentence for the murder of Stephen Cameron in 1996 in Swanley, Kent. The tip-off that led to Noye's arrest is believed to have come from Joe Wilkins AKA Lucifer.

Joe Wilkins was named as the 'introducer' for Operation Cotton, a police sting operation in Spain. According to the Guardian newspaper, "Judge Bathurst Norman, throwing out cases against 10 men, ruled that there had been "massive illegality" and illegitimate entrapment. The police had set up a fake investment company and, using Wilkins to make introductions, lured criminals to place £15m "black" money with them, an operation which they saw as the cutting-edge of crime fighting but the court regarded as improper." Other reports say the "black" money came not only from British criminals on the Costa del Sol, but also drug operations in North Africa (including Colombian businesses) and money laundering in Gibraltar.